VENGEANCE

Rebel Sons MC Book 2

Gracie Williams

Between the Covers, LLC.

ISBN: 9798324595012
Independently published by Between the Covers, LLC.

Cover design by: Between the Covers, LLC.
Library of Congress Control Number: 2018675309
Printed in the United States of America

CONTENTS

TRIGGER WARNING

This book contains mature themes and is intended for those at least 18 years of age. This story includes references to:

Abuse- physical, sexual, and emotional.
Physical Violence
Human Trafficking
Gun Violence
Kidnapping
Profanity

VENGEANCE

PROLOGUE

Anna

I jolted awake to the muffled sounds of shouting and commotion outside the steel door of the room I've been locked inside. For months, the only noises had been the occasional footsteps of the guard bringing scraps of food and water. But this? This was different.

A spike of fear mixed with hope lanced through my weakened body. My heart thundered in my ears as I strained to make sense of the escalating noise. A distant rumbling vibrated the bare concrete beneath me, the tremors growing until the floor itself seemed to be quaking.

Then the roar of gunfire erupted, deafeningly loud even through the thick steel door and concrete block walls. This was it. I was about to die in this waking nightmare, just like Michael always promised. I shrank back against the dingy cot, every muscle rigid with terror.

It was a struggle just to remain still, let alone try to move. Every movement sent excruciating pain radiating throughout my body. Each breath felt like shards of glass scraping against my broken ribs. The dull ache in my head pulsed in time with my heartbeat. It took all of my willpower to open my swollen eyes, and when I did, the world spun around me.

The sound of gunfire grew louder and closer, until it was interrupted by rough cries and loud thuds right outside my door. The sharp smell of burnt gunpowder filled the stagnant air, making me wince.

The door was hit with a powerful force, causing it to shudder violently and let out a bone-jarring metallic groan. The hinges screeched in protest as the impact came again and again, until the door finally burst inward with a deafening crash.

I instinctively threw my hands up in a fruitless attempt to protect myself as I lay on the small cot. After what felt like eternity, my eyelids fluttered open again to see a towering figure filling the doorway. He stood easily over six feet tall, with large muscular arms straining against his white shirt that hugged his chest tightly. His unkempt dark blonde hair framed a ruggedly handsome face. The intense gaze of his blue eyes seemed to pierce right through me.

Reflexively, I attempted to retreat. Yet my malnourished frame, reduced to mere skin and bones from months of starvation, lacked the strength.

The man's face held a fierce, almost animalistic intensity. Others might have been frozen in fear by his threatening presence, but after enduring months of torture and abuse at the hands of real animals, he didn’t frighten me. I felt surprisingly calm in his presence.

"Jesus Christ." He mumbled, as he took in the state of my body. My muscles were weak and thin, clinging onto my bones, and my colorless skin was covered in bruises. I could only imagine how frail and broken I must have looked to elicit such a reaction from this man.

The burly stranger swiftly moved to my side and gently placed his worn leather vest over my frail, exposed body. I couldn't help but flinch at his sudden proximity, but the mix of cologne and exhaust somehow brought a sense of comfort.

He effortlessly lifted me in his strong arms. Despite the gentleness of his touch, the pain still shot through my body like a bolt of lightning. I couldn't help but cry out as he lifted me, each movement causing a new wave of agony to wash over me. My tears fell freely as I clung to him.

“I’m sorry sweetheart,” he spoke in a hushed and gentle tone. “Judging by the looks of you, I can’t imagine a damn place I could touch you without hurting you. You call me Rex, you're safe with me. Your mom and Sarah have been worried about you." My mind raced.

He knew my mom and Sarah?

He abruptly turned and marched down the dimly lit hallway. The rhythmic sound of his boots on the floor was soothing, lulling me to sleep. I fought to keep my eyes from closing, wanting to ask about Sarah.

Just then, a voice that I thought I would never hear again pierced through the fog of sleepiness in my mind, bringing back a flood of memories and emotions.

"Anna! Oh my god... Anna!"

It couldn't be her, but it was. It was unmistakably, the panicked voice of my dearest friend, my sister, calling out to me. Sarah.

It was all my fault that Michael found her. The guilt and shame ripped through me as I thought about how my weakness had led to her being here.

As we stepped out into the sunlight, fresh tears flooded my eyes. The brightness was almost too excruciating to bear after spending so much time in the darkness.

My savior shifted me in his strong arms, one hand cupping the back of my head gently as the other cradled my wilted form protectively against the hard plane of his chest. His heavy boots carried us quickly up the sidewalk to safety as I struggled to keep my eyes open. Fighting against the undertow of sleep trying to pull me under yet again.

I felt him transferring my limp body into the back of an awaiting van. Through my fading vision I saw Sarah's tear-stained face appeared before me. She leaned in close, her trembling hands softly running through my hair as she whispered in my ear. I wanted to apologize. Tell her how sorry I am that she ended up here in this hell because of me. But consciousness was quickly slipping away from me.

Rex carefully positioned me against his chest, as if I were made of delicate porcelain. The intense fire in his eyes from earlier had faded into a gentle concern, with no hint of hostility left behind. Instead, I could see a profound tenderness shining through his gaze.

As the van started to move, his rugged features came into clearer view. I caught bits and pieces of his low, gravelly voice as he muttered something that I couldn't quite make out. Just the sound of his deep timber and the vibrations low in his chest brought a sense of comfort. He shifted his massive frame to hold me closer, radiating a strong and reassuring warmth into my weakened body.

In my weakened and traumatized condition, it should have been comical to feel safe and protected by him. He was a massive, intimidating figure whose very appearance screamed "danger" to any logical person.

And yet, in those last few moments of consciousness, this time I felt no fear as the darkness swallowed me. Instead, an unfamiliar feeling of protection blanketed me as I sank deeper into all-consuming blackness. Despite every expectation I had that I was going to die in that room Michael had locked me inside, Rex had freed me. He was my salvation.

As I gave in to the bone-deep exhaustion crashing over me, there were no echoes of past tortures waiting for me. No agonizing flashes of pain or screams ringing in my ears. I was free from degradation and suffering. Only the gruff, fallen angel's physical presence amidst the chaos. The memory of his searing yet inexplicably gentle gaze boring into mine. The feeling of being utterly safe and shielded from harm, for the first time in my life.

CHAPTER 1

Rex

The hospital room was dim, with only the soft beeps and whirs of medical equipment breaking the silence. I pulled the uncomfortable chair closer to Anna, studying her weak, battered body.

Her sunken cheeks and eyes appeared even more pronounced against her pale skin, pulled taut over her gaunt face. I traced the maze of tubes and wires emerging from her thin hospital gown, delivering vital fluids and nourishment to her emaciated form.

The evidence of her extensive injuries was present all over her body. From the dark bruises that covered her face to the splints supporting her fingers. The thick bandages that wrapped around her torso were still visible underneath the thin hospital gown she wore. The doctors had solemnly informed Sarah and me about the countless ways she had been harmed and the cruelties inflicted upon her.

She had fractured ribs and facial fractures. Her abdomen was sliced open, infected to the point of almost killing her. When I found her, she was lying on a dirty cot, delirious and naked. My anger flared at the thought of how close we had been to almost being too late.

Without even realizing it, my hands formed tight fists. My blunt nails digging into the rough skin of my palms as the memories replayed in my mind. Her vacant, lifeless eyes and how shocked I was at how unnaturally light and fragile she felt as I carried her to the van. A shudder coursed through me, but I quickly suppressed it.

I don't do emotional bullshit well on a good day, but the sight of her lying so broken and demoralized, it gnaws at me in a way I can't quite put words to.

It's a brutal reminder of the unconscionable inhumanity that we are all capable of. The unimaginable cruelty and pain humans can inflict upon each other. A harsh reality that this world shows no mercy, whether it takes innocent and kind souls like Anna, or leaves them in peace.

I've learned this lesson the hard way, more than once. Losing my wife Becky and our unborn son shortly after Em was born was a devastating blow. It all happened in an instant, with one careless mistake snatching away two of the most important pieces of my life.

I tried to save them, reached for Becky with everything I had as her car crumpled under the impact of the semi barreling through the intersection. I could only watch helplessly as her eyes dimmed, her hand going limp in mine in those final agonizing moments. Gut-wrenching losses and regrets I'd give anything to somehow rewind, but I'm stuck living with the shitty hand that life dealt, and I helped create.

Sarah and Jake think my lingering presence in Portland is just some bullheaded need to stand guard over Anna. To be here for her and them in case old man Moretti retaliates for killing his son and torching his chop shop where their trafficking ring operated out of. I gave my dad a half-truth along those lines about not leaving Jake shorthanded, playing on his concerns over the family to justify my staying here.

The truth is, I'm not sticking around just to protect Anna and my family in case that Moretti fucker comes looking for payback. It's more than that. I feel responsible, like I owe it to her to see this through. Walking away now, while she's still putting the pieces back together, trying to claw her way out of that black hole she almost didn't make it out of. I don't know, something about that just doesn't sit right with me.

I can't explain it, but I have this strong need to be by her side through this. To make damn sure she pulls through. I refuse to let her choose any other path. No one lives through that kind of hell just to give up and die after finding a way out.

Maybe it's purely fucking selfish. Like I'm trying to earn some kind of absolution. But I won't bail on her, not until I know she's gonna be alright.

It's like I owe it to Becky's memory to save Anna since I couldn't save her, as twisted as that sounds even to myself. Something deep inside is driving me to stay by her side, a persistent tug in my chest that defies all logic or understanding. All I know is that I'm not leaving this place or her side until I see the clarity and spark of life return to those eyes.

So, I keep holding vigil night after night, fitfully dozing in the cramped recliner that looks child size compared to my massive frame, in her room more out of necessity than preference.

The first few days of her hospital stay she seemed empty and detached, trudging through an endless waking nightmare even though her body was physically safe behind these sterile white walls. Her screams would pierce through the night with horrifying regularity, echoes of the psychological torment she'd endured at the hands of those sadistic fucks. I'd station myself outside her room, fists balled at my sides while she thrashed and fought against invisible demons.

On those nights, I couldn't help reliving my own wife's final moments strapped helplessly in the mangled wreck. I don’t think the memories will ever stop feeling like jagged shards of glass tearing at my insides. Becky's face ghostly pale and smeared with blood. Her lips moving in an eternal silent scream even as I shouted for her to hang on. The acrid stench of gas and burnt rubber, the shriek of twisting metal as the semi plowed into us. Blinding headlights careening towards us, Becky's scream of my name cut abruptly short by the impact. I'll never shake the bone-deep guilt of failing to protect them or stop seeing Rebecca's face the moment she took her last breath.

Regrets and loss like that changes a man, tempers you with bitterness and hard-edged resilience. It's the kind of pain that never completely fades, just gets brutally compartmentalized in order to function from day-to-day and keep moving forward.

She doesn't need pity or feeble, misguided coddling, the kind of soft reassuring bullshit most people would try consoling her with. Anna's strong enough to recognize that placating shit for what it is, I see it in the flickers of clarity gradually illuminating the shadowed depths of her eyes. She needs an unwavering, steadfast presence by her side, a beacon to guide her through the suffocating darkness threatening to consume her.

Coarse one-sided banter about the dumbassery of my club brothers or the headaches of tinkering on my bike out in the lot. My meaningless conversation fills the void of time as she floats in and out of a dazed state of consciousness. It's devoid of any sugary empty platitudes or trite motivational speeches. Just a solid, reassuring constant for her to latch onto when being awake becomes too much to bear. When reality is just too overwhelming, too intense, and the memories too real. I'm there for her when her mind needs something solid to focus on amidst the chaos.

Make no mistake, Anna's well of fortitude clearly runs deep if she can claw her way back to the land of the living after the hell those twisted fucks put her through. As each day passes, I watch as the emptiness in her piercing dark eyes fades away, I see glimpses of who she really is begins to resurface and reclaim its place. With each day of learning more of who Anna is, a peculiar feeling stirs low in my stomach. A mix of pride, respect, and an indescribable connection to her that I struggle to put into words.

When our eyes lock, I can feel a tender warmth emanating from her gaze. It's as if an unexplainable bond, an invisible thread of understanding, is forming between us. I have no idea how to make sense of it, but something inside me tells me not to fight it. I'm just not sure if I can do that.

For nearly eight weeks, I have been gently guiding Anna out of her shell, pleading with her to come back to the present and escape from her never-ending nightmares. As we sit in her dimly lit hospital room tonight, it feels like the thick fog clouding Anna's mind is finally lifting.

“Rex…” as she says my name, her slender fingers fidget against the stiff white hospital sheets. Without thinking, I reach out and hold her hand in my own rough, calloused one. Her bones feel delicate and fragile beneath my grasp, like a bird's.

“Thank you.” She speaks with a broken voice, tears threatening to spill over. I can see the immense gratitude she holds, unspoken words weighing heavily on her delicate features.

Feeling uneasy by the heavy emotions shining in those dark copper-flecked eyes staring intently into mine, I let out a reassuring grunt and give her hand a firm squeeze, trying to ground us both.

"Don't mention it, sweetheart. Just save that pretty voice of yours for more important shit than thanking me, yeah?" I aim for an easygoing chuckle, shooting her a lopsided grin despite the roil of emotions churning in my gut.

I might not know what to make of this newly formed friendship with Anna. I do know I’m not walking away from her.

CHAPTER 2

Anna

After eight weeks in the hospital, I gaze out of the van's tinted window and watch as the Rebel Sons compound comes into view. It rises from the rugged Montana terrain like a fortress nestled among tall pines and rocky peaks. My heart races with a combination of fear and relief, knowing that I will finally have a safe place to let my guard down after enduring a life of captivity and last few months of torture.

The vehicle rolls past the imposing perimeter fences lined with strands of razor wire, one of the guards giving us a curt nod as we approach the main gates. I take a steadying breath, Sarah's warm presence beside me in the backseat providing a small degree of familiar comfort amidst the sudden uncertainty I feel.

As we drive through the central compound area, the van finally comes to a stop in front of a row of attached townhomes. Rex kills the engine of his massive Harley, the throaty rumble falling silent as he dismounts with a casual grace and rounds the van.

The door swings open, filling the dim interior with blinding sunlight that has me squinting against the assault on my senses. His large hand closes over mine with gentleness as he leans in close.

"You're safe here, sweetheart," he murmurs, blue eyes holding my gaze with an unwavering intensity. "We're on our home turf now. No one's getting through those gates unless we want them to."

I can't stop the sudden hitch in my breath at the endearing term slipping so effortlessly from his full lips. Despite his tough demeanor, there's a clear sense of protectiveness in Rex's voice that has become a constant source of comfort for me. I squeeze his hand gently before accepting his help out of the van.

As soon as my feet touch the smooth pavement of the driveway, we are greeted by Beau, Rex's father, and the President of the Rebel Sons MC. He exudes an air of authority; his mere presence demands respect. I can't help but feel a bit intimidated by him.

Beau and Rex bear a striking resemblance to each other. They are both tall, massively well-built men with piercing bright blue eyes that seem to see right through you. Where Rex still looks youthful at 35, Beau has a distinguished charm about him with his striking silver fox looks.

Beau stands among a group of large, muscular men that instinctively make me want to shrink back. However, Rex's hand moves from my wrist to the small of my back, his comforting presence calming my desire to shy away.

Beau and I exchange brief introductions before he gestures for me to follow him. As I turn to look back at Rex with a worried expression on my face, I feel my heart race with anxiety. But his silent nod is an unspoken encouragement that I can do this. I don't have anyone or anything to be afraid of here. With Sarah following closely behind, I command my shaky legs to move forward and catch up with Beau as he makes his way through the crowd of bikers.

I let out a sharp breath as we stop in front of one of the rustic townhouses. I recognize the woman standing frozen staring back at me on the front porch. She's a little older now since the last time we were allowed to see each other but still just as beautiful. Beau puts a reassuring hand on my shoulder, "Sophia has been waiting a helluva long time for this kid. I'm sure you have too."

Dark curls frame her stunning face as tears cascade down her cheeks. She looks me up and down taking in my every detail with rapt eyes.

"M-Mom?" I can't quite believe my eyes, believe that this isn't another cruel joke constructed to torment me. But then she is rushing forward with a broken cry, pulling me into a fierce, achingly familiar embrace. Her flowery scent crashes over me in waves of long-suppressed memory from the handful of supervised visits I was permitted during my youth.

"My Anna, my sweet Anna..." she croons in my ear between wracking sobs, her fingers splaying against the back of my head in a gesture of pure, unbridled relief and profound tenderness. All I can do is cling back just as desperately, blinking against the sting of tears scalding my eyes.

Over my mother's shoulder, I find myself instinctively seeking out Rex where he lingers back among the other club members. Perhaps sensing my silent plea for reassurance, he gives me a subtle nod of acknowledgment. Knowing that this is a profound and long overdue moment for me and my mother, one he seems content to respectfully witness at a distance.

* * *

Night falls over the compound and I find myself sitting across from my mother at the kitchen table and listening as she recounts years of the Moretti family keeping us apart through a toxic slurry of intimidation and explicit threats against my life and hers.

"I never stopped loving you, Anna," she vows, emerald eyes blazing with a righteous fury that still simmers beneath the surface. "Not a single day did I ever gave up hope that someday, somehow I might get to bring you home to me where you belong. Safe with me."

My throat constricts as she speaks, her words overflowing with a deep sadness that she has held back for so long. I reach across the table and gently take hold of her trembling hands, feeling the rapid beat of her pulse beneath her delicate skin. It's a tangible reminder that this is not another cruel dream, but a real moment that we are both experiencing together.

"Tony and his thugs will never understand the fierce love between a mother and her child," she seethes, drawing on all the horrifying tales of her torture under the organization. "I endured everything, just to keep fighting for you... and my only regret is not being able to shield you from their brutality."

I try to comprehend the immense amount of pain and tragedy my mother has faced in her 41 years of life. She was kidnapped as a young girl, destined to be traded for drugs with a Mexican cartel. My father, Tony Moretti, had other plans and kept her for himself. She endured sexual assault and abuse until she became pregnant with me. She was forced to bear a child while still just a child herself.

Thinking of the torment my mother, Sarah, and I all have suffered through at the hands of those vile, greedy men cause fresh tears to prickle in the corners of my eyes. The small kitchen starts to blur as the harsh edges are softened into a hazy impression of pastel shadows dancing on the hardwood floors and light-colored walls.

A creak of a floorboard behind me causes me to quickly turn my head towards the entryway, my body tensing with the instinctual fight-or-flight reaction that has become ingrained in me. Relief washes over me when I see its Rex. He's standing in the open doorway with his large frame and broad shoulders taking up the entire space. I feel a twinge of embarrassment at being scared so easily. I should feel secure here, surrounded by people who have sworn to keep me safe.

"You two need anything?" Rex's gravelly voice breaks the silence. I scan his chiseled face for any signs of emotion, but his stony expression remains unchanged behind the tattoos on his neck and scruff covering his jaw.

"I think we're good, Rex," Sophia speaks gently as she stands up to give Rex a maternal hug, which he awkwardly accepts and then quickly detaches from. "I appreciate everything you've done for us, Rex. I can never repay you enough for bringing my Anna back to me."

Just knowing Rex is nearby lessens the overwhelming anxiety

that ripples through me when I am left alone with my scattered thoughts for too long. Despite my efforts to keep them locked away, deep fears still lurk in the shadows of my mind.

My fear is like a relentless monster constantly hunting me down. No matter how hard I try to escape, I can’t. It seems that I needed my own monster to stand up for me. To fight the monsters still locked inside that won't leave me.

* * *

I wake up the next morning just as the sun starts to peek through the curtains. Unable to drift back to sleep, I get out of bed and wrap a plush robe around my body before stepping onto the front porch. As I take in the view, the gentle breeze caresses my skin.

I relax into one of the comfortable deck chairs, I hold a steaming mug of coffee and allow myself to just be in this moment. The sun slowly rises over the distant Montana horizon, casting a sense of peace and calm all around me. My tired mind and body soak up the sights and sounds of this beautiful place like a desert oasis drinks in a rare rainfall.

As the rising sun slashes golden tendrils across the tree line, a door opening and then closing draws my attention away. Rex catches my eye as he exits his house next door. He stretches his muscular arms up above his head, then plants his booted feet firmly on the ground.

I take in Rex's chiseled features as his gaze meets mine, his eyes narrowing against the bright morning light as he openly gives my appearance a thorough once over. I try to muster a half-hearted smile, a small hint of the genuine ones I used to have. His typically surly expression softens ever so slightly as he regards me with an unreadable look.

"Mornin', sunshine," Rex drawls in his trademark gravelly timbre. "Good to see some color back in those cheeks. Guess this mountain air is agreeing with you."

“I guess breathing in fresh air is a bit of a step up from the stale, musty, basement air I am accustomed to." I toss back in a lighter tone than expected. Rex grunts out a soft scoff, one thick eyebrow winging upwards in what could almost be interpreted as amusement if one were feeling generous.

“You got plans for today?”

“Yeah, I’m going to hang around here with mom today, she goes back to work tomorrow. Did you need something?”

“No sweetheart, I didn’t need anything. Just making sure your raggedy ass isn’t planning to slack off the rest of the day." He flashes me a playful grin.

Some might find Rex’s words harsh, but I understand that he’s just making sure I’m not going to lay in bed and retreat inside my head with all the monsters. It’s his way of making sure I’m moving forward and not stuck in the past. He’s showing he cares without coddling or holding my hand. Pushing me to move forward with my own strength. Not relying on him or anyone else to do it for me.

Ever since he carried me out of that basement, this is exactly what I've needed and exactly what he's done. Rex was only willing to carry me while I was too weak to do it myself. This is his way of showing me I'm strong enough now to do it on my own.

CHAPTER 3

Anna

That fragile sense of comfort and inner calm lasts through the first few days of settling into my new daily routines under the watchful eye of the club. I find myself reveling in simple freedoms and pleasures that were so long denied to me. Taking long, hot showers that feel like baptisms. Fresh air filling my lungs with each inhale, delicious food that my body craves after being deprived for so long.

Despite the temporary peace I find during the daylight hours, as soon as night descends, my body is overcome with tremors and cold sweats. I am plagued by vivid nightmares that leave me thrashing and whimpering in a state of panic, my sheets and clothes soaked with sweat. Each night brings a new terrifying dream to pull me under like a riptide.

A loud knock on my bedroom door startles me out of my sobs and silences my cries. I know without a doubt that it's Rex as he steps into the room, his wide frame taking up most of the doorway and blocking out any light or movement from outside. He looks at me with a deep frown and concern etched on his face, taking in my frail state as I lay curled up in a ball in the disheveled sheets.

"You here with me?" Rex's deep voice resonates through me,

calming the chaotic flood of nightmarish images that plague my mind.

I nod, my throat feeling tight as I forcefully exhale a long, shuddering breath and struggle to regain my fragile hold on reality. For some reason, the steely, unyielding depths of Rex's eyes bring me back from the brink of oblivion that the cruel bastards had pushed me towards. As I breathe in deeply, the details of the room gradually come back into focus, and the hold of the nightmare loosens with every ragged breath.

Rex strides across the room cautiously with deliberate steps and sits down on the bed without hesitation. His weight causing the mattress to dip beneath him. The intense heat radiating from his skin immediately engulfs me, making my clammy limbs feel like they're on fire.

Before I can process the situation, his rough hand is gently pushing away the strand of damp hair clinging to my forehead. As his fingers trace down the sharp line of my jaw, trying to soothe me with his touch.

I nearly let out a whimper at Rex's tenderness, a stark contrast to his hulking and rough exterior. My heart beats wildly against my throat as he moves closer, his scent of sandalwood and worn leather engulfing me and overpowering any urge to run.

"Just breathe, Anna," he murmurs softly. He’s so close to me now that each warm breath of air caresses my tear-streaked cheek. "Match my breaths, in and out. Don't let your mind get ahead of reality. It’s just me and you. I won’t leave your side."

Rex has a talent for effortlessly transitioning from the

formidable and dangerous aura he projects to one of sincere compassion and tender care. His ability to adapt like a chameleon never fails to amaze me. He has a carefully crafted facade that he shows to his brothers in the club, and to most other people. A sturdy layer of toughened armor that he uses to protect himself. But when he's with me, or with his daughter, I see the mask slip, the armor crumbles away, revealing his true self. He is a beautiful man, inside and out.

* * *

In what I've figured out is Rex's way to distract me and get me out of my own head, he will ask me to go on a walk with him after Emmalynn has gone to bed. Each time it ultimately turns into us walking over to the large garage on the compound. It houses the fleet of semi-trucks the club uses for their transport business. In one of the far back corners of the garage, he works on a small, rusted go-kart frame he is restoring for his daughter, Emmalynn, for her birthday.

I find comfort in observing the skillful movements of his large, calloused hands as he takes off and adds pieces and parts with the same focused determination that I've grown used to seeing in his daily interactions. Rex doesn't lecture or offer dramatic speeches as he works; just fun banter and simple, casual conversations about anything and everything.

One evening about a month into my stay at the Rebel Sons compound, out of the blue, Rex began to share some of his past with me.

"I lost my wife, Rebecca. Few years back now." He keeps his head angled down over the dismantled go-kart, but I see the hairline fractures webbing across his stone face. The minuscule muscle tics playing around the edges of his full lips as he swallows hard enough for his throat muscles to jump.

"Car wreck, it was my fault. My fuck up that ended with her dead, and me trying to figure out how the fuck I was going to raise a kid on my own. Em started crying, me being a first-time dad and never around kids much, I overreacted to every noise she made. I took my eyes off the road for just a second, but it was enough time to ruin all our lives, and get Becky killed along with my son she was carrying. No one knew she was pregnant but me." Rex pauses, nodding to me, "and now you."

Rex continues in a gravel-toned rasp, his knuckles whitening around the greasy tools gripped in his hand with increasing force.

"Semi driver blew through a light on the highway. T-boned Becky's car, dead center. Didn't even have time to hit the brakes because I was turned around trying to make sure Em was okay."

I feel the breath still in my lungs, suspended in the weighted pause as Rex lets the implication of his trauma hang in the air between us like a physical presence. His jaw works in a harsh clench before he draws in an audible inhale through flared nostrils.

"Em... Emmalynn was barely six months old." His gaze remains downcast but the wetness glistening at their corners doesn't go unnoticed.

"Managed to get Em out of her car seat in the back and into my arms."

I shudder as he speaks with such raw emotion and shares his vulnerability with me in this unguarded moment. My gut instinct urges me to turn my body towards him, fully facing the intense anguish that he has been holding back. I brace myself for whatever haunted details he is about to share with me.

When our eyes connect this time, Rex's bright blue gaze is glassy and assailed by ghosts.

"I held her... held Em up to Becky's face right up until she stopped breathing. I held her hand in mine so damn tight. Like I could keep her with us as long as I didn't let go. I watched the light fade from her eyes. Heard her last wheezing gasp as everything we'd built got ripped away in the blink of a fucking eye. Part of me died inside that mangled car alongside her."

"Oh god, Rex." He stops me from saying anything further with a shake of his head. Fresh tears slide down my cheeks as empathy wells up inside me for this complex, brooding man sitting beside me but seeming to exist in a different world all of his own right now.

Rex continues in a low rasp, the greasy wrench gripped tightly in his palm he was using.

"Just wanted you to know, I know how guilt feels, how it can eat away at your insides until there's no you left. Until you're nothing more than shame and regrets. Can't ever let it go completely, even when you know in here it wasn't your fault." He moves his grease covered hand up to tap the side of his head with his index finger.

“You have nothing to feel guilty about, Anna," Rex’s words ring with conviction. It’s as if he can read my thoughts and see all the turmoil inside me. Our eyes meet, a silent exchange of understanding passing between us. It’s like we’re both baring our souls to each other like open wounds.

“Rex, he broke me because I was too weak. I told Michael where Sarah was because I couldn’t take it anymore. I couldn’t take the pain. I couldn’t take another cut from his knife. Another one of his men...”

My voice trailed off; I couldn’t bring myself to finish the sentence. I hadn’t told anyone what happened to me in that basement. How the guards repeatedly used my body any way they wanted. I was ashamed, humiliated, and disgusted with myself. How would everyone else feel about me if I felt that way about myself? I couldn’t bear seeing a look of disgust on Rex’s face every time he looked at me if he knew. So, I continued on hoping he wouldn’t ask any questions.

“My weakness got not only her, but Jake’s sister, and poor little Barrett kidnapped too. That’s my nephew Rex. I should have given my life to protect that little boy and keep him safe. But I didn’t because I was too weak. All three of them could have been killed and it would have been on me. Them being taken is on me. All because I wasn’t strong enough for them.”

"I see the guilt you carry around Anna. I’ve watched you drown in it since I carried you out of that basement. You survived Anna. You got Sarah out of a fucked-up situation that she probably wouldn’t have survived. That’s what you focus on.

What you're not getting through your goddamn head is that it wasn't on you to stay strong enough for them. You had to stay strong enough for you. To stay alive, to save yourself. You did what you had to do to survive. To make sure you made it out of there breathing and not in a fucking body bag.

It doesn't matter what you had to do to survive, it only matters that you did. Anna, you made it out because you are strong, and I respect the fuck out of you for doing it. Now all that's left is to keep living. Putting one foot in front of the other and moving forward without. It's the only path left, and the only one I'll allow you to take."

As he speaks, I feel a weight lifting, a release of the burden I've been carrying. It's not absolution, but rather a reminder that this struggle, this constant battle with my inner demons, is not one I have to face alone, no matter how lonely it may seem in my darkest moments.

Rex is a living testament to the fact that one can be completely shattered to their foundation and yet still have the strength and determination to stand tall. Maybe that's why his presence has brought such a sense of comfort and safety to me. It's not in spite of his rough exterior and intimidating demeanor, but because of them. They serve as guideposts mapping the harsh terrain, we're each struggling to navigate.

CHAPTER 4

Rex

Every week, Friday was the day I looked forward to the most. Em and I had a routine. Every Friday I picked her up from preschool and we would spend the evening together making pizzas and watching movies. A little tradition just for the two of us.

As I pulled up to the school in my truck, I couldn't help but think about asking Anna to come over tonight. It sure as hell wasn't easy convincing her, but she eventually gave in. Anna has avoided being around anyone else at the compound besides her mom, Sarah, Jake and me. I'm hoping Em will be okay with Anna joining us and that Anna will feel comfortable in our home.

Em came bounding out when the dismissal bell rang. I couldn't stop the grin from stretching across my face as a familiar brown pigtailed blur barreled straight toward me, tiny sneakers scuffing across the concrete.

"Daddy!"

Emmalynn launched herself at me, and I caught her effortlessly, her little arms winding tight around my neck. Pressing a smiling kiss to her rosy cheek, I was surrounded by her sugary baby scent mixed with hints of grass.

"There's my best girl!" I gave her a squeeze, never taking these moments for granted knowing I never had any time with my son. I'll take every moment I can get with Em, good or bad.

"Hi daddy! It's Friday, that means pizza! Pizza! Pizza!" she chanted, sky blue eyes sparkling with excitement.

Chuckling, I swung her little body to settle her on my hip.

"You know it, kiddo. But before we go home, I need to talk to you about something. You remember when daddy had to go away to help auntie Sarah and Cass, and then I stayed to help my friend that got hurt?"

She nodded solemnly. "Uh huh, I missed you, but you made sure Grandpa Beau maked the pizzas with me! He burned them the first time and he made me promise not to tell you we just ate the ice cream for dinner."

"Of course he did." Brushing a kiss to her temple. "I missed you too, baby. More than you know. But I'm back now, and my friend that was hurt is feeling better."

"The pretty lady with the owies on her face?"

Damn, she was too perceptive for a five-year-old sometimes. Em didn't miss a thing. I smiled tightly and nodded.

"That's her. Her name is Anna and… she's had a hard time lately. She's been really sad."

“Anna," Emmalynn echoed carefully, as if committing the name to memory.

"That's why I asked her if she would come over tonight for pizza night. I thought maybe you could cheer her up a little bit. Help put some smiles on her face. What do you think? Would you be okay if Anna had pizza night with us?"

For a moment, Em seemed to seriously ponder it. Then that sunny smile lit up her pretty little cherub face.

"Yeah! I can make her feel better! Oh, I know! She can paint with me! That always makes me happy when I'm sad."

I squeezed her tighter, so proud of this incredible little girl, and relieved that maybe I’m not screwing up too bad raising her on my own.

"That's a great idea, baby. I think Anna would love that. Just one more thing I need to talk to you about." I opened the truck door and set her in her booster seat.

"You might notice some owies on Anna's face. Maybe some other places where she got a booboo that's still healing up, okay?" My hands were gentle as I strapped her into the safety harness.

"So, we're not gonna say anything about those owies, or stare at them. That could make Anna feel really sad again. You got it, Munchkin?"

Emmalynn zipped her lips solemnly and nodded, “got it daddy.

I'll make her lots of happy." Thank fuck she's an awesome kid. She made this single dad thing easy on me.

Three hours later, my hoodie littered with errant flour streaks from our pizza prep, I heard the sharp rapping of knuckles at the door. I smiled as Em squealed and scampered down the hallway.

"She's here! She's here!" Her tiny feet pounded against the wood floors, accompanied by a chorus of giggles that floated back toward me.

"Anna! Anna, Anna!" Emmalynn chanted as she launched herself at Anna for a hug.

Pure shock painted Anna's features as Em's little arms wound around her legs. For a split second, Anna looked like a cornered animal, body going rigid with fear. Then her body visibly relaxed, and she tentatively patted Em's back. Our eyes met over the top of my daughter's head, and my chest constricted at the sheen of tears shining in Anna's eyes. Swallowing hard, I gently pried Emmalynn off our guest.

"All right, Em, let's not smother the poor woman."

That coaxed a faint smile from Anna and seemed to dissolve some of the tension in her shoulders. Small wins.

"Hi Anna!" Em crowed in between us. "I'm Emmalynn but you can call me Em for short! I'm 5," she holds up five chubby little fingers for Anna to see. "I made a picture for you!"

She ran over to the coffee table and snatched up a piece of

colorful artwork, tiny legs pumping as she rushed back over. Anna bent down as Em proudly presented the crayon sketch of two stick figures. One bigger with long dark hair for Anna, the smaller one with brown scribbles for hair for Emmalynn, beside a smiling sun.

“See Anna, we are friends.” Em points to the picture she drew of the two of them.

"Oh wow..." I heard Anna murmur, seemingly at a loss for words. Her fingertips drifted over the childish figures reverently. "Em, it's beautiful. Thank you."

"Do you like it?" Em looked thrilled that her gift was appreciated. "We're gonna have a fun pizza night an' watch movies! I'm gonna make sure you're not sad no more, ever. It’s my job, we are friends now!"

Smiling, Anna curved her arm around Emmalynn's little shoulders and pulled her into a warm embrace. "You are already doing great at your job, sweet pea."

And just like that, the lingering shadows weighing down those gorgeous eyes lifted. It was like Em's light chased them away, if only for a little while.

“Hey Anna." I sauntered closer, with what I hoped was an easy grin to cut through any remaining tension. "Glad you could make it. And thanks for braving the energizer bunny over there." I jerked a thumb back toward my still bouncing daughter.

"No thanks needed..." Her gaze flickered between Em and me,

a well of unreadable emotion briefly welling behind her eyes before clearing. "I'm always up for some good company."

"Well, you're in luck!" Swooping down, I scooped Em up into a fireman's carry, grinning at Anna over my shoulder as my daughter unleashed a squeal of laughter. "This is the very best company in town. Only top-notch goofballs accepted."

"Was that a compliment or an insult?" Anna replied dryly, arching one slim brow.

I simply shrugged in response before carting my wiggling child back toward the kitchen.

"Pizza awaits Princess. Your culinary services are needed."

Over the next hour, I stood on the sidelines watching in amusement as Em led Anna through the entire sacred pizza making process in the most serious of tones. Clearly in charge of the operation.

"Now you stretch the dough like this, 'kay?" Em demonstrated by valiantly attempting to fling a circle of dense dough over her tiny head. "We got to get it nice and flat."

As the dough promptly flopped back down, half draped over Em's face, I cringed. But Anna didn't miss a beat, retrieving the doughy flap and lightly flicking Em's nose with it.

"Like this, you mean?" She deftly spun the dough aloft with one hand until it ballooned into a wide, flawless circle, before depositing it effortlessly back onto the baking stone with a charming lopsided smile.

Em froze mid-giggle, mouth agape as she blinked up at her new friend turned Pizza Master.

"You... you're a witch!" she accused, awestruck.

I couldn't stop my snort of amusement at her exclamation, or the way Anna's shoulders shook as she swallowed down her own laughter. Her eyes twinkled when they found mine over Em's head.

"Oh dear," Anna replied solemnly with an easy and elegant flourish of her dough slinging skills. "You've found me out. A witch indeed. I promise not to cast any evil spells on you. Maybe, on your daddy though."

I bit back another burst of laughter because I knew exactly what Anna just unknowingly stepped into. My only response was a broad grin and a salute of my beer as Emmalynn immediately launched into a thousand and one questions about proper pizza witchery.

I stood there in my kitchen taking in Anna making pizza with my daughter. She looked lighter, I'd never seen her look happy before. My gaze traced the lines of her profile as she swiped a loose lock of brown hair from her brow. Her cheeks were slightly flushed from laughing, pink lips curved up at the corners. When her eyes landed on mine, their color shifted between different hues of brown in the kitchen's warm lighting, and something inside me shifted too.

The sudden awareness that this woman, despite the hardships and demons she carried, was fucking beautiful. Not in that cold, hard, plastic way so many women manufactured themselves into. No, her beauty was natural and soft.

Lost in my thoughts, I was suddenly being pelted with doughy projectiles that left flour smeared across my shirt. Another glob of flour-coated dough hit me squarely in the chest this time, and I stared at Anna in betrayed shock.

"You'd better start running."

She didn't have to be told twice. Snatching up a double handful of doughy ammo, she shrieked and bolted from the kitchen with me in hot pursuit.

Emmalynn's laughter rang out behind us as she eagerly hurled fistfuls of the stuff at our retreating backs.

Anna made it as far as the living room before I snagged her by the wrist and spun her into my chest. She landed against me with a breathless laugh, immediately dissolving into helpless giggles as I relentlessly pelted her with the dough bombs.

"Okay! I give up!" she squealed through her laughter, feebly trying to fend off my projectile attack.

I paused, grinning down at her flushed, smiling face so near to mine. Something hot and electric surged in my veins at our sudden closeness, her body soft where it pressed against mine. She sucked in a shaky breath, her laughter petering out as her widened eyes locked with mine. There was a question in their molten depths, an invitation, or maybe just surprise at her own body's response.

I opened my mouth, not even sure what I planned to say. But then Em's squeal sounded behind me followed by a face full of flour.

"Sneak Attack!"

Sputtering, I released Anna and spun to see Em doubled over in a fit of giggles, cradling her belly.

"Oh no you didn't!" Scooping her up, I tossed her over my shoulder while she squealed in delight. All awkward tension dissolved in the wake of her infectious laughter. Glancing over my shoulder, I found Anna watching us with a tender smile.

I called back to Anna, "Get the oven preheated, witch. There will be time for revenge later."

* * *

The movie's closing credits rolled across the screen, the flickering glow casting everything in a soft blue tint. I stole a glance at Emmalynn nestled between Anna and me on the sofa. Her eyes were hooded, those long lashes fluttering as she fought a losing battle against sleep. With a tender smile, I drank in the sight of her sweet face, so much like her mothers.

Emmalynn's breathing gradually slowed and steadied. I

carefully scooped her up in my arms, feeling the comforting weight of her body against my chest. Her face nestled comfortably against the curve of my neck. From the corner of my eye, I noticed Anna observing my every move.

I carried my precious cargo down the dimly lit hallway toward her bedroom. I gently laid Emmalynn amid her stuffed animals and rumpled blankets. Brushing the deep brown hair back from her face, "goodnight princess, sleep tight."

Leaving Em's room, I found Anna in the kitchen cleaning up. When she heard my footsteps behind her, she turned, "you two really get into pizza night. How long have you two been doing this?"

I took a deep breath, leaning my weight into the kitchen island behind me.

"You know I thought the day we lost Beck, or the day I had to bury her while holding my six-month-old daughter would have been the hardest days of my life. They were the worst, but not the hardest.

Every milestone Em hit, all of her firsts. First steps, first tooth, first birthday, those were all the hardest. Knowing Beck should have been the one here for all those firsts, she deserved to be the one still here. Knowing Em would be so much better off with Beck raising her than me trying to half ass my way through it.

Emmalynn's first day of preschool, I was so ate up on the inside with guilt that Rebecca wasn't here to see her. To see how much she's grown, what an amazing kid she is. I was so sad for Em that she didn't have her mom there and wouldn't her entire life.

I took that from both of them.

When I came home after dropping Em off that day, I was in a bad place. I was reaching for a bottle of Jack I had stashed when I spotted Becky's old recipe box on the shelf, right where she'd left it." Clearing my throat, I pressed onward.

"When I opened it, one card fell out on the counter. She had written "Friday Night Pizza" at the top of the card. It had a recipe for sauce on the front and dough on the back. Beck loved to make pizza it was her favorite.

So instead of getting shitfaced like I had wanted to, I went to the grocery store. Made sure I had everything Beck had wrote on the front and back of that card. Then Em and I started making pizza every Friday night. The only Fridays I've missed are the ones I spent in Portland. I made sure my dad did pizza night with Em while I was gone. I don't know, I just thought I owed it to Em and Beck for them to have something together even though they never had the chance."

One corner of my mouth tugged upward in a sad approximation of a smile as I glanced up.

"You wouldn't believe the disasters that were our first attempts," I admitted with a raspy chuckle.

"Poor Em tried so hard to be a good sport about it. But we both knew it was terrible. After a few more failed efforts, we made a pact. We wouldn't give up until we had perfected her Mama's pizza, no matter how many tries it took."

Out of the corner of my eye, I registered the expression playing across Anna's features. I saw the apology forming before it could pass Anna's lips, that telltale tightening around her eyes and mouth as tension gripped her slender frame. My stomach clenched in anticipation of the retreating I knew was imminent. What I didn't expect was the moment Anna threw her arms around me.

"You shouldn't have been away from Emmalynn for so long because of me," she whispered, wrapping her arms tightly around my midsection. "Those lost moments with your daughter... they're something you can never get back. I selfishly took that from you, and from her."

"No." The word emerged on reflex, flat, and unyielding enough to halt her self-recriminations in their tracks. I watched a tiny crease furrow between Anna's brows as confusion displaced the apology.

My hand moved on its own, drawn to the delicate curve of her jaw. Her eyes widened as I guided her gaze to meet mine, silently begging her to understand what I was about to say.

"Don't you dare take that on, Anna," I said hoarsely, my thumb tracing the soft skin along her cheekbone. "Those were my choices to make, do you understand? I was exactly where I needed to be... where I wanted to be."

Her throat bobbed as she swallowed hard, those fawn-like eyes glistening with unshed emotion in the low light.

"But Em--"

I tried to reassure Anna, "Emmalynn was fine. Safe and happy with my dad and grandma Marlene. She loves spending time with them." I spoke firmly, leaving no room for argument.

"They were over the moon to spoil her while I was gone. Don't beat yourself up about it. You don't have a damn thing to feel bad about."

I must've said the right thing because she studied my face intently before giving a slight nod. Her acceptance, that little bit of trust, seemed to break through a barrier between us. In that moment, the small space separating our bodies felt incredibly noticeable.

Close enough for me to see the light freckles scattered across the bridge of her nose. Close enough for her shaky exhales to brush against my skin. Close enough for that undeniable pull between us to intensify tenfold.

Instinctively, my free hand drifted up until my fingertips hovered an inch from Anna's cheek. The small scars still healing were more pronounced up close, faded yet lasting reminders of her strength despite the unbearable ordeals weighing her down.

In that frozen moment, I could barely breathe past the knot of conflicting longing and fear tightening my throat. Part of me ached to close that final gap between us, to wrap my arms around Anna's delicate frame. To shield her, somehow, from the demons still lingering behind her guarded eyes. Yet another insistent part warned me to tread carefully, or I might inadvertently do more harm than good and send this beautifully broken woman retreating behind her sturdy wall she's built.

My hand hung there between us, caught in limbo. Part of me wanted nothing more than to close that distance, but fear stayed my movements. What was the right move here? I searched Anna's eyes, hoping for some sign. Then it hit me, simple truth that put things in perspective.

"Listen," I said, my voice low and serious. "Whatever went down back there, it doesn't change how I see you. Not one bit."

Anna's eyes snapped up to meet mine. She looked almost afraid yet hopeful at the same time. Like she wanted to believe me but wasn't sure if she could.

"You're pretty fucking tough, you know that?" My voice held a gruffness, but also unmistakable reverence. I reached up, gently tracing a slightly raised scar under her eye.

I searched her face, looking for any discomfort. Anna just stared back; lips parted slightly as she breathed shakily.

Maybe I couldn't save Anna single-handedly. That was a battle only she could win. But I'd be damned if I didn't fan those smoldering embers back into an inferno. I could do that much after she persevered through the unspeakable.

The sound of the backdoor shutting and approaching footsteps from the hallway jolted us apart like an electric shock. I snatched my hand back as if burned, whirling to face the unexpected intrusion.

In the doorway stood my dad, Beau. “Didn’t mean to interrupt, just wanted to let you know we have church in the morning. Jax has some intel coming in, thinks he'll have it all by morning to share at the table."

"Uh, I should probably go." Anna's voice sounded strained behind me. I turned to see her hugging her arms tightly across her chest, closed off.

"Anna, wait-" I tried, but she just shook her head wordlessly and slipped past me and Dad, clearly retreating.

"I gotta go. Sorry."

The muffled thud of her socked feet faded down the hallway as she made a hasty exit, leaving an awkward tension in her wake. I dragged a hand through my hair, unable to meet my father's scrutinizing stare.

The disapproval rolled off him in waves, his stance rigid. I could feel his eyes boring into me, demanding an explanation.

"Don't start dad." I muttered. I couldn't bring myself to look at him.

Of course, my dad knew me too damn well to just let it go. Rocking back on his heels, he arched an expectant brow.

"I didn't say a word, son." And that was exactly the problem. He didn't need to say anything. The weighted silence spoke volumes. I kept my eyes trained on the floor, suddenly self-conscious under his paternal x-ray vision.

"Fuck." The crass utterance slipped out before I could stop it. "I don't know what I'm doing here. With Anna, with any of this..." My hands clenched into fists at my sides, fingers flexing as if seeking a physical outlet.

"One minute I'm just trying to help her find some comfort, help her dig out of that hole she buried her mind in to protect herself in that basement.

The next minute, it was like... like I crossed some line, you know?" I scrubbed my palm over my jaw, feeling the rasp of stubble.

"There is this pull with her, this magnetic awareness that just seemed to click into place out of nowhere. It's the way I felt when I first met Rebecca and it's scaring the shit out of me."

My dad stayed silent, simply letting me get it all out at my own pace. After a long stretch, I blew out a harsh breath and chanced a look at him. "I can't get that close to her, dad," I confessed in a low rasp.

"You know it nearly broke me when I lost Beck," I rasped out. My jaw clenched as those memories hit me, a despair so all-consuming, I truly didn't think I'd ever climb out of it. "I can't survive that again. I won't make it through a second time."

I tipped my head back, squeezing my eyes shut, fighting for control with each ragged breath. When I could finally meet my dad's gaze again, his expression had softened slightly around the edges. He seemed to study me for a long moment before responding.

"Listen, son," he said gruffly, but with unmistakable tenderness underneath. "Moving forward, starting a new chapter... that doesn't take away one bit of the love you had for Beck, you hear me?"

The weight of his words hung between us as I let them sink in, turning them over like a lifeline.

"I know better than anyone just how big your heart is. You feel deeply, you always have since you've been little. That's not a bad thing, Rex. It makes you a great father, a great son, a great brother. Becky wouldn't want you closing yourself off like you have. She wouldn't want your last chapter to end when her's did. You're 35 years old, you still gotta whole lot of life left to live."

I opened my mouth to protest, but he lifted a hand to stop me. "Now I'm not saying to charge ahead without caution either," he cautioned sternly, holding my gaze. "That girl... she's been through holy hell, more than anyone should ever have to, truth be told. She's gonna need a gentle hand and whole lot of patience to help piece her back together."

Dad seemed to wrestle with his next thoughts. "But I'd be lying if I said she wasn't already benefiting from having you in her corner. The way she pulls herself out of that dark place when you shine a little light into those shadows?" A ghost of a proud smile tugged at the corners of his mouth. "That's a rare gift to be able to give to someone, Rex. Not one to take lightly."

"So, what are you telling me, dad?" I finally managed to ask. "What should I do here?"

Something flickered across his face, there and gone too quickly to name. Suddenly, he looked every one of his 51 years, worn yet unbreakable.

"Way, I see it, you got two choices ahead," he said in a deliberate drawl. "You can lock the gates up tight and never let another soul in. Spend whatever years you got left shuttered away, safe in your ways, but you'll die a miserable old bastard." He left the implications hanging with a weighted pause. When I stayed silent, dad continued.

"Or you can take a deep breath and see where this twisted road leads you." His sharp gaze bored into me with intense focus. "It won't be an easy road to follow. More than a few twists and bumps along the way. You just gotta be ready to weather whatever comes without falling apart again.

No matter your choice, I'll back your play. But I'd be lying if I said I don't hope you'll at least consider going to see where this new road could lead you. Might turn out to be your best ride yet."

CHAPTER 5

Rex

I sat stone-faced in the chapel as Jax filled us in on the intel he's been gathering.

"Tony Moretti has put out a five-million-dollar bounty on Anna's head." His voice echoed through the room, cutting through the silence like a razor.

"He wants her silenced. He has put the word out he will pay dead or alive, as long as she is delivered to him either way."

Jett, our club secretary, let out a long whistle. "You sure about that number? Five million is a fuck of a lot for one chick."

Anna had just found a glimmer of hope, a chance to rebuild her life. Now, that hope was hanging by a thread.

"This is bad," Talon, the club's road captain, drawled. His voice laced with concern. "Really fucking bad. For a chance to get their hands on that kind of cash? There will be some heavy hitters gunning for her."

I sat seething with anger. How dare Moretti or any other mother fucker treat Anna as if she were just another item to be bought or sold? How could a man assign a value to their kids' life like they are just another disposable asset. Fuck him.

"We need to make sure her and Sophia stay on the compound grounds," Pops said, his voice gruff. "Low life sacks of shit like Moretti wouldn't think twice about using someone close to Anna to get to her."

Jax nodded. "I've already got Sophia's shifts at the Ridge covered and set her up with a laptop so she can still manage what she can from here."

"We'll do whatever it takes," I vowed. Anna was under my protection now, and I would do everything in my power to keep her safe.

The only thing on my mind was making damn sure Moretti, or anyone else didn't get their hands on Anna. All the healing she'd done, the work she's put in. It would all be for nothing, right down the fucking drain.

She is just starting to mend her scars. The bond between us was new, yet I couldn't picture my world without Anna in it anymore. I won't allow some piece of shit like Tony Moretti to take her away from me. I can't lose someone close to me again. Not fucking happening.

I sat, fists clenched, as everything really sank in. A multi-million-dollar bounty on Anna's head? What the hell had that woman done to deserve a target painted on her back? What does she know?

"Moretti must know something we don't," I growled, my mind racing. "What could she possibly know that would make her worth five million dollars to him? Anna's been through enough hell. I'll be damned if I let that bastard get his hands on her."

Jax shook his head. "That's the thing Rex, I can't find any trace of Anna or her involvement within the Moretti organization. I can't find any trace of Anna at all. There was never any type of birth certificate, no school or medical records, no financial or work records as she got older. She's never existed anywhere except within the walls she's been confined inside by her father and her brother her entire life."

"So, what are we gonna do about it?" Ox demanded, his gruff voice cutting through the tension. "We can't just sit on our asses while that psycho's got a price on her head."

Beau leaned forward, his eyes narrowing. "We find out what the hell is going on. Jax, I want you to keep digging, keep us informed on anything else you find. Where is Anna now?"

Jake, my cousin and our club's enforcer, spoke up. "She's at my place, with Sarah and Barrett."

Beau nodded, sending a text on his phone. Within seconds the door to the chapel opens, all of our eyes shifting to Park, our youngest prospect standing in the doorway.

"Park, get your ass over to Jake's place and escort Anna back here to the chapel. Make sure she knows she's safe with us."

I grabbed my phone as soon as my dad gave the order, typing out a quick message to Anna.

> *Me: Hey, everything's fine. The club needs to ask you some questions. Parker is coming to walk you over to the clubhouse, but I'll be waiting for you. Don't worry, you're safe.*

I hit send, hoping it would help ease any panic she might feel at Park's sudden appearance. The last thing I wanted was for her to feel threatened or unsafe here at the compound with us.

When the chapel doors opened and Park entered with Anna, my heart clenched at the fear etched on her face. Her eyes were wide, lips parted as she scanned the room full of hardened bikers. I shot up from my seat, meeting them at the door.

"Give us a minute," I said gruffly, wrapping an arm around Anna's shoulders and guiding her back out into the hallway.

Once the door closed behind us, I pulled her into my embrace, her trembling body melting against mine. "Hey, it's okay," I murmured, cradling the back of her head, her dark brown curls wrapping around my fingers. "You're alright, sweetheart. I've got you."

Anna nodded against my chest, her breathing ragged. "I was so scared when Parker showed up. I thought..." She swallowed hard.

"I don't know what I thought. It's just when you said the club wanted to ask me questions. It made me panic. Michael hurt me for so long asking questions about where Sarah was. I know you aren't like him." She nods her head towards the chapel door, "I know they aren't like him, but I still can't stop the panic I feel."

Cupping her face, I stared into those deep brown eyes. "You're safe here, Anna. I promise you that. But we need to figure out why that sick fuck of a father of yours has put a bounty on your head."

Anna's face went pale. Her delicate features frozen in a mixture of shock and confusion. "A bounty? On me? But I haven't done anything."

"I know. That's what we're trying to find out." I brushed my thumb over her cheekbone. "You ready to go in there? I'll be right beside you the whole time."

Anna gave me a hesitant nod, and I gripped her hand tightly in mine. Opening the door to the chapel, I led Anna inside. I pulled out a chair for Anna, at the far end of the table. She sat opposite of my dad, who sat at the head of the table as President.

I squeezed Anna's hand reassuringly as we took our seats. Her eyes darted around nervously at each of my brothers surrounding us.

Beau cleared his throat.

"Anna, thank you for talking with us. We just need to ask you some questions to try and figure out why Tony has put that bounty on you."

She nodded, a tremor in her voice. "O-okay."

"You said you've been confined by Michael and Tony your whole life," Jax started gently. "Did you ever overhear anything? Any conversations. or see documents that could give us a clue as to what you might know?"

Anna worried her bottom lip, as she searched her memories. After a tense moment, she spoke up.

"Like what exactly? Tony made one of his men teach me to how to handle his books and do accounting work for his businesses. So, I've seen some accounts and things like that."

A sudden realization hit me like a ton of bricks, leaving me breathless. If these businesses were illegal, their accounting books would be too. I couldn't even begin to imagine what kind of incriminating information those numbers held.

"Accounting work?" Wyatt raised an eyebrow in question. "What kind of businesses was he having you do the books for?"

"There were three main business. Then there were a few that are just fronts." Anna admitted hesitantly. "But there were always multiple sets of numbers and accounts I had to balance. A lot of cash transactions with no real documentation."

Jax's eyes narrowed. "Sounds like he was cooking books to me. Hiding money trails and income sources."

"Which could mean any number of illegal operations," Gunnar added grimly. "Drugs, guns, human trafficking... the possibilities are endless."

Anna's already pale face went white as a ghost, her hand tightening around mine.

"Oh god, I was never told where the money came from, I swear. I was just taught how to cover it up."

Leaning forward, I caught her gaze with mine.

"Hey, you didn't know what you were doing. You were just following orders from that sick prick."

I shot a look around the table, daring anyone to disagree. To my relief, nods of agreement came from the other members.

"Rex is right," Gunnar affirmed. "You can't be held responsible for the shit they forced you into. But those books could be the key to taking down Moretti's whole operation."

A heavy silence hung in the air as we all processed the possibility. Anna could unknowingly hold the evidence to dismantle her father's criminal empire. No wonder he wanted her eliminated at any cost.

I pulled Anna's chair closer, wrapping a protective arm around her shoulders. She leaned into me, her body trembling.

"It's gonna be okay," I murmured, pressing my lips to her hair. "I've got you; I'm not letting anything happen to you. The club won't let anything happen to you. We all have your back Anna."

I watched the tension ripple across Anna's gorgeous face as the weight of the situation settled over her. Beau leveled his gaze at her from the head of the table.

"Anna, I know this is a lot to take in, but we need your help," he said, his deep voice calm but firm. "Would you be willing to work with Jax and Gunnar? Try to explain exactly what you were made to do with those books?"

Anna's eyes flitted to me, and I gave her hand a reassuring squeeze under the table. She drew in a shaky breath before nodding.

"Yes... yes, of course. Anything I can do to help."

Beau's expression softened slightly. "Jax here is a goddamn wizard when it comes to digging up information on people and their dealings. And Gunnar, he's our treasurer, a numbers guy through and through. Between the two of them, we should be able to start piecing together what those books contained."

Leaning forward, I brushed a stray curl from Anna's face.

"You don't have to be afraid, sweetheart. We've got you, and we're not letting anything happen to you." My gaze hardened as I looked around the table. "That's a promise."

"Damn right," Talon growled from across the table, his jaw set. "Moretti wants a war. He's got one."

Gunnar moving his attention back to Anna, "Anna, you feel up to getting started on this today after Jax and I are finished here?"

"Sure, I can do that."

I squeeze Anna's hand again to get her attention.

"Will you be okay waiting out in the common room until we are finished in here? Shouldn't be too long. Park is out there too if you need anything."

"I'll be okay Rex."

I reach behind me and open the chapel door and yell for Park. He's there within seconds, the kid is eager to earn his patch.

"Take Anna out to the common room and stay with her until we are done here. Get her whatever she wants while she waits."

After Anna left the room, a silence fell over the chapel as the reality of the situation sank in. We were gearing up for an all-out offensive against one of the most powerful criminal organizations in the country. But I knew without a doubt that my brothers would stop at nothing to protect Anna, to protect our family, to protect what was ours.

Beau's voice rang out, steely determination in his tone.

"Listen up, sons. We're going to war. That prick Moretti made a big fuckin' mistake putting a price on one of our own." His eyes bored into each of us. "I want everyone ready to move at a moment's notice. We're not stopping until we've blown apart

Moretti's whole goddamn empire."

A rumble of agreement came from my brothers around the table.

"Jax and Gunnar, you two work closely with Anna," Beau orders. "Get every bit of intel you can from her. She's the key to this whole operation."

Jax gives a curt nod, already focused on his laptop. Gunnar's eyes are alight with determination. He was born to tear apart numbers and financial records.

"X and Wyatt you're with Jake at the garage this week," Beau continues. "He's got a backlog of custom builds and mods he needs help powering through." He turns his steely gaze to me.

"Rex, you and I will be in to lend a hand where needed at the garage. But first, I've got a skip that needs bringin' in. Take Dom with you. Time for the prospect to start learning the ropes if he wants that patch."

A slow grin spreads across my face at the prospect of some action. It's been too long since I had a good chase and takedown.

"Yes sir," I reply, giving my dad a nod.

"Jett, Ox, and Talon, you're on transport duty," Beau rumbles. "Haul runs are light this week, so if you're not behind the wheel, you're in the garage pitching in. Everybody clear?" A chorus of affirmatives rings out. "Good, get out of here and handle your shit."

As the chapel clears out, and I make it out into the common area, I catch Anna's eye from across the room and give her a reassuring nod. She's the key, the one thing that could bring Moretti's whole house of cards crashing down.

I make my way to Anna, sitting beside her on one of the leather sofas in the common room. Anna turns those big brown eyes up to me.

"Rex... what if I can't remember enough? What if I've put you all in danger?" I stared at her with an intensity that left no room for doubt.

"You listen to me. You didn't put anyone in danger, we all signed up for this. After we found out about the trafficking ring, every chapter within the Rebel Sons voted to take them down.

This was going to happen regardless, with or without you. Whatever you can tell us will help. You were asked to help us and that's what you're doing, helping us." I pressed my forehead to hers, my voice a low rumble.

"I'm not letting anything happen to you again, you hear me? We're gonna get through this together. You and me."

Anna's lips parted; her breath shaky as she searched my eyes. Then, slowly, she nodded.

"Together."

CHAPTER 6

Anna

Gunnar leads the way into the basement under the clubhouse. I take a deep breath, steeling myself as I enter.

"Jax has been working on building this command center for a few years now." Gunnar motions for me to enter the room in front of him.

Jax gives me a reassuring nod as I approach the bank of computer monitors displaying a dizzying array of financial data and coded information.

"Anna, we need every shred of information you have on how the Moretti's operate from the inside," Gunnar says, his intense gaze boring into me.

"Tony had me set up shell companies and offshore accounts to launder money." Jax's fingers fly over the keyboards as I rattle off names. Crestview Construction & Development, Regali Imports, Santoro Family Vineyards are all fronts for funneling illicit funds.

"The cartel drug shipments would come through those businesses, disguised as legitimate imports or construction materials." I pause, my throat tightening. "I never knew how the Cartel was paid until Rex told me. I was never forced to do anything with trafficking. They would have had to kill me; I wouldn't have done it."

Gunnar's jaw tenses, then starts explaining to me how the exchange worked.

"The cartel demanded payment in human cargo. Young women, sometimes children, were sent across the border by your brother in shipping containers, sent to Mexico as compensation for the drugs."

My stomach churns learning those horrors, but I force myself to press on, revealing every detail I can recall. If there's any chance to bring my father's empire down, I have to try.

Pointing to Regali on one of Jax's monitors, I explain how my father used it to smuggle drugs inside shipments of Italian ceramics and marble from overseas suppliers.

"The containers would come through the Port of Los Angeles, hidden among the legitimate cargo. Vito Trinci oversaw the operation there."

Gunnar leans forward, listening to every word as I recount masking money trails through overinflated construction invoices and slush funds at Crestview Construction.

"Paulie Ciccio ran all the construction projects. They'd pad the material costs, siphoning off funds into offshore accounts."

Jax rapidly types, making notes about offshore accounts used to launder profits from Santoro's wine distribution. His eyes laser-focused behind black-rimmed glasses.

I list off account numbers burned into my brain, routing details for wire transfers, any financial accessibility I was given into the Moretti's' system. Providing access codes and passcodes I still remember, Jax's eyes widen as I reveal shortcuts to bypass security encryption.

I describe the cash deposit boxes stashed in basement walls at Regali. I feel Jax's eyes burning into me as I divulge, Stephen Molinari, the Santoro regional distributor, had a hidden vault in the wine cellar at Santoro with backup data on every transaction and more cash they haven't laundered yet. Gunnar scribbles down the locations preparing for their assault.

Gunnar stares at me a moment, looking... impressed?

"Explain to me the process you were taught to maintain two sets of books." Taking a breath, I describe the intricate reverse data entries, flipping signs, reallocating costs to mask totals deemed risky.

"We'd shift losses into shell companies, burying them under layers of phony invoices and transactions. That way, the top-line numbers always looked clean on the financials we filed."

Seeing Gunnar's approving nod, I swell with confidence, realizing my unique skills just may be what the club needs to take down the entire operation.

Gunnar crosses his arms, listening to everything I have to say as I lay out detailed breakdowns of revenue allocations across the syndicate's various operations.

Gunnar stands tall and imposing, just like every other member of the Rebel Sons. His broad shoulders and muscular build seem like it fills the entire room. His light gray eyes shine like a piece of polished steel. His dark hair is cut short but still messy in a way that makes him better looking. His tattoos peek out from under the rolled-up sleeves of his flannel shirt.

"Keep going," Gunnar urges, leaning in. "We need to bleed these bastards dry from every angle."

I dive into the complex formulas used to disguise cash flows from the drug trade under inflated wine distribution invoices. Describing how I'd bury money trails in cost-of-goods data for the ceramic imports.

"The Regali shipping containers were a gold mine for hiding drug cash. We'd inflate the customs valuations ten-fold on the manifests, then skim the difference into offshore accounts."

Jax's fingers fly across the keyboard, eyes narrowed intently as I rattle off account numbers and routing details. I feel a surge of adrenaline coursing through me, fueled by the chance to bring down the twisted empire that enslaved me for so long.

Pulling an old ledger from my bag, I flip through pages covered in intricate coded entries only a few people within the Moretti organization could decipher.

"This is one of the only things I brought with me when we stopped at Michael's house before we left Portland to pack my things. I forgot I had it, it was in a stack of books I grabbed in a hurry. I was thinking maybe there is something in here you guys could use?"

As Gunnar pores over the book's complex columns and numbers, his eyes narrow, clearly understanding the implications.

"What do the initials M.H. stand for?" Gunnar asks.

"That is Mr. Hidalgo. He did some importing for one of the businesses. I met him a few times."

Jax stares at me in disbelief, "Are you talking about Mateo Hidalgo? That's the leader of the Garza Cartel who your father was sending trafficked girls and women to."

I feel my stomach drop. "I didn't know who he was, just that he met with Michael a few times for business. Sometimes it was with Michael's boss from the D.E.A."

Gunnar shakes his head, "That confirms our theory about Michael joining the D.E.A. to protect their drugs being brought into the country from the inside."

Over the next hours, I systematically lay out everything I was forced to learn about the syndicate's financial infrastructure. Detailing import-export scams, insider trading, embezzlement from legitimate businesses they controlled. No matter how deeply buried or intricately disguised, I reveal every illicit income stream and shady accounting trick I can remember.

Jax's systems visualize the entire sickening scope of my father's empire, nodes and connections linking like a circulatory system. Occasionally he pauses me to ask for clarification on some archaic laundering method or encrypted data vault.

"Walk me through the offshore holding companies again," Jax says, adjusting his glasses. "How did they filter profits from the drug trade?"

I inhale and take a moment to recall the complex network of fake entities that were used to hide illegal money transfers.

"We'd layer transactions through multiple pass-through accounts in the Caymans, Luxembourg, Cyprus... wherever had the loosest reporting requirements. Disguising the money as interest income or investment returns from legitimate real estate deals."

Gunnar shakes his head in disgust. "Greedy pricks were lining their pockets from every angle."

I nod and continue to reveal the details of the elaborate scheme that funnels rigged corporate profits into personal slush funds. I disclose the names of silent partners and corrupt accountants who were paid to turn a blind eye.

"Your dad didn't send you to school but did teach you to be a criminal mastermind, didn't he?" Gunnar's mouth twists in a mixture of disgust and impressed awe.

"My father had his accountants groom me to be his unwitting accomplice from a young age. I was just a pawn in his twisted game." Pushing aside the lingering trauma, I steel my resolve. "But now, I get to turn the tables and dismantle everything he's built."

Gunnar gives my shoulder a reassuring squeeze. "You're one tough broad, Anna. The way you've persevered..." He shakes his head in admiration.

Jax taps a few final keystrokes, analyzing the data web I've helped map out.

"Anna, this is huge. You gave us more than we expected you could. With your knowledge, we can cut off their money pipelines and choke the entire operation." His eyes meet mine with an intensity that makes me shiver. "You're our secret weapon against them."

I feel a surge of determination, finally able to strike back at those who've caused so much suffering. "Good. It's time they felt a little bit of pain instead of everyone else around them."

"You did good today kid," Gunnar 's praise fills me with a sense of accomplishment. "Now, you get to witness the downfall of your father's empire, and you'll get the satisfaction of knowing that you were the one that burned the fucker to the ground."

CHAPTER 7

Rex

I leaned back in the van seat, my eyes scanning the small house across the street where our skip is holed up inside. Beside me, Dom fidgets restlessly, drumming his fingers on the dash.

"Relax, kid," I muttered, giving him a sideways glance. "Dude ain't going nowhere."

My phone buzzed, and I pulled it out to check the message.

> *Gunnar: Anna killed it today. Girl's sharper than a straight razor. We're making serious headway. Jax is eating it up, I think he's in love.*

> *Me: Glad to hear it. Keep me posted.*

A satisfied smirk tugged at the corner of my mouth. Despite the hell Anna had been through, she was still standing tall, doing whatever she could to help bring down that prick Moretti. Her strength was admirable, to say the least.

I felt a sense of pride knowing she was safe back at the

compound, working alongside the brothers. With every lead she provided, every money trail she helped uncover, we move one step closer to ending this shit for good. With Anna's help, we were going to bleed Moretti dry and make that bastard pay for every ounce of suffering he'd caused. She was a fighter and having her on our side was a game-changer.

Dom's foot is tapping impatiently on the floorboard beside me. "Why're we just sitting here with our dicks in our hands? Let's snatch this bitch up already." I snicker at the prospect's eagerness, shaking my head.

"Some things never change. Patience there, Sparky. I'm just trying to do this the easy way and avoid shit going sideways upfront."

I killed the engine and turned to face Dom; his eyes wide with that eager puppy-dog look rookies always had bringing in their first few skips. Couldn't blame the kid though, I remembered that rush all too well.

"Alright, listen up," I said, keeping my voice low. "This ain't our first rodeo with this lowlife, his name is Dale. Few months back, Jake and I scooped him up on a prostitution charge. Stupid son of a bitch jumped bail again after getting pinched in another hooker sting."

Dom nodded, hanging on my every word like it was the gospel truth. I fought back a smile, kid had a lot to learn, but at least he was paying attention.

"From what I remember, this guy's just your typical IT nerd. Scrawny, awkward, probably spends more time jerking off to anime porn than getting any real action." I paused, letting that imagery sink in for dramatic effect.

"But don't let that fool you, dude's still a slimeball. Just because he ain't built like a linebacker don't mean he can't be dangerous if he's cornered." Reaching across the console, I grabbed the spare set of cuffs and tossed them to Dom.

"Soon as we get in that door, you slap those cuffs on him. I'll take point, you hang back and cover our exit. We get him secured and it's a straight shot back to holding. No detours, no pit stops. You got me?" Dom swallowed hard but gave me a confident nod.

"Got it, VP. I'm ready." I clapped him on the shoulder, flashing a wolfish grin.

"That's what I like to hear, prospect. Just follow my lead and stay alert."

With that, I shoved open the van door and stepped out onto the pavement, Dom falling in step behind me as we approached the house. Just another day at the office.

I pounded on the front door with a heavy fist. The moment Dale cracked it open and caught sight of my face, I saw the flash of recognition in his eyes. He didn't say a damn word, just slammed the door closed. Then the sharp click of the lock followed.

I stood on the weathered porch grinning, the wood creaking beneath my boots as I rapped firmly on the door again.

"Come on, Dale, don't make this difficult on yourself. You know you're going in today, so just open the door so I don't have to break it down and you don't have to pay to have it fixed. You got twenty seconds to make your choice."

The seconds ticked by, and when Dale failed to comply, I drew back my leg and drove my boot into the door, the wood splintering as it gave way under the impact.

I was barely inside the threshold when a blur of motion caught my eye, and I barely had time to react as Dale came barreling out of a nearby closet, a toy lightsaber clutched in his hand. The cheap plastic smacked against my shoulder, and I let out a surprised chuckle.

"Are you fucking shittin' me, Dale?" I growled, shaking my head in disbelief.

I felt a sharp, stabbing pain rip through my body like a bolt of lightning, every muscle seizing up as I crashed to the floor in a heap. It was like being swarmed by a thousand angry bees, their stingers piercing every inch of my skin. I couldn't move, couldn't breathe, couldn't even think straight as the agony consumed me.

Through the haze of pain, I could just make out the blurry shapes of Dale and Dom standing over me, their voices muffled and distant. I blinked hard, trying to force my eyes to focus as the sensation slowly began to ebb away.

"Are you ok big guy?" Dale's nasally voice cut through the fog, dripping with mock concern. "You should probably consider going back to your old partner, this guy seems to be a dumbass."

The sharp crack of Dom's hand connecting with the back of Dale's head echoed through the room, followed by the prospect's frantic apology.

"Shit Rex, I'm sorry," his eyes wide with panic and maybe a little fear. "I was aiming for Captain Star Wars over here."

I gritted my teeth, my fingers twitching as the feeling slowly returned to my limbs. I could feel the rage bubbling up inside me, the urge to lash out and make them both pay for this humiliation. But I forced it down, taking a deep breath and pushing myself up to my knees.

"You fucking TASED me?" I snarled, my voice a guttural growl ripped from deep within my chest. Turning all my attention to Dom, who seemed to shrink under the intensity of my gaze.

"You better pray to whatever god you believe in that you didn't just permanently fuck up your chances of ever getting patched in."

Turning my sights on Dale, he shrank back, the plastic lightsaber clattering to the floor as he held up his hands in surrender.

"Hey man, I was just defending myself! You broke down my door!"

"Don't give me that bullshit!" I roared, taking a menacing step forward.

"Get your ass down on the floor and don't fucking move." He

opened his mouth to protest, but the look on my face must have stopped him cold. Slowly, he lowered himself to the dingy carpet, his eyes darting between me, and Dom. Dom swallowed hard, his Adam's apple bobbing.

"I- I'm sorry VP, I didn't mean to hit you, it was an accident!" I take a deep, steadying breath, clenching and unclenching my fists as the tingling sensation finally started to subside.

"Take this piece of shit out to the van," I growled, jerking my chin towards Dale. "And give me that goddamn taser."

Dom didn't need to be told twice. He scrambled to yank Dale up off the floor, slapping the cuffs on him with shaky hands before hauling him towards the exit. I could see the fear in his eyes as he handed over the taser, no doubt wondering what fresh hell I would unleash on him for this.

"Sorry," Dom mumbles sheepishly as he's walking out with Dale in tow. I shoot him a withering glare but say nothing.

My eyes catch sight of that ridiculous plastic lightsaber lying on the floor. Scooping it up, I give it a once over, picturing the look of pure joy that would spread across Emmalynn's face when I surprise her with it.

I walk out of the house and gesture for Dom to toss Dale into the back. The scrawny bastard lands with a pained grunt, glaring up at me with those beady eyes.

"Hey, that's mine!" he whines, reaching out with cuffed hands towards the toy lightsaber still clutched firmly in my grip.

A low, rumbling chuckle escapes my throat as I lean in close, my lips curled into a taunting smirk.

"No Dale, it was yours. Then you decided to be a pain in my ass and got me tased by dumbshit over here." I jerk my head towards Dom. "And now it's mine. You wanna try to take it back from me?"

Dale opens his mouth to protest further, but one menacing look from me is enough to make him quickly reconsider. Smart move on his part.

Sliding the van door closed with a heavy thud, I take my spot in the driver's seat, the lightsaber resting in my lap. My fingers trace over the cheap plastic ridges as I picture Emmalynn's bright, toothy grin when I hand this over to her. A small smile tugs at the corners of my mouth at the thought. Those little moments of joy are what make the shit I have to deal with bearable.

Glancing over at Dom, the kid's a fucking mess of nerves right now, no doubt dreading the ass-chewing he's got coming his way. *Good.*

I pull in front of the clubhouse, killing the engine, I swing open the driver's side door and hop out, snatching up that ridiculous plastic lightsaber before slamming it shut again. I make my way towards the clubhouse entrance, Dom trailing a few paces behind me with his head hung low like a kicked puppy.

The moment we step through the doors into the common room, every pair of eyes turns our way. X is the first to speak up, a shit-eating grin plastered across his face.

“I heard you had quite the experience teaching the prospect the ropes today," he says with a smirk, giving me a knowing glance.

A rumble of laughter rises up from my other brothers scattered around the room. I shoot X a steely glare, but it only seems to spur them on further.

"We should probably let someone else teach the kid seeing how you got your ass handed to you." Talon calls out, prompting another wave of raucous laughter.

My cheeks flush with anger, and I can feel my jaw clenching so hard that it's surprising my teeth don't break. But before I have a chance to retaliate, my father's rough voice booms into the room.

"Rex! Get your ass in here!" Spinning on my heel, I storm towards the President's office, the laughter and jeers fading into a dull roar behind me. I shove open the door with a little more force than necessary, not even bothering to knock before taking a seat across from him.

"Gunnar talk to you about Anna?" Dad asks, leaning back in his chair. I nod, the plastic lightsaber still clutched in my hand.

"Said she killed it today. Really helped move things forward against Moretti." My dad lets out a low whistle.

"She did more than good, Rex. Gunnar said she's a goddamn genius at finding ways to launder money and then hide it, one of the best he's ever seen."

My eyebrows shoot up in surprise at that. I knew Anna was sharp, but for Gunnar, a seasoned vet when it came to finances, to sing her praises like that. That was no small feat.

"We were thinking about offering her a job with the club," dad continues. "Gunnar has more work than he can handle. If she can free up some of his time with the accounting for the club businesses, then he can help out more in the garage and on transport runs."

I think it over for a moment, rolling the idea around in my head. On one hand, having Anna's skills on our side would be a massive asset. But part of me also worries about piling too much on her plate when she's still so fragile. Dad must sense my hesitation.

"What do you think? I wanted to ask you about it before we spoke to her. I don't want her to think she has to take the job; she's not being forced. It's a job offer. I don't want to put more on her than she can handle either. I know she still has a long way to go in her recovery."

I let out a slow exhale, mulling over his words carefully. Part of me feels fiercely protective of Anna, not wanting to see her get overwhelmed or pushed too far too fast. But I also know how much purpose and drive she's shown in wanting to take down Moretti. Maybe having an official role to play, could be just what she needs.

"It's been almost three months since we found her. Physically, she's mostly healed. Mentally, she's still got some work ahead of her. I'll talk to her about it. If she's up for it, I think it's a smart move," I say finally. "Let her decide if she's ready to take that on."

"My thoughts exactly, son. If she's up for it, I'll have Gunnar explain the job, see if she's interested. If she is, we'll get her settled in and make sure she's got everything she needs." As I rise to head out, dad's voice stops me.

"Oh, and Rex?" I pause, turning back to face him with a quizzical look.

"Try not to get your ass kicked by any more nerdy hipsters with toy weapons today, yeah?" He flashes me a teasing grin. I level him with a flat glare, fighting back a smirk of my own.

"Yeah, yeah. Real fuckin' hilarious, old man."

The rumbling of laughter that erupts from my dad's chest follows me down the hallway and through the clubhouse doors.

I tuck the lightsaber under my arm as I make my way up the paved drive towards the townhouses. My Gram, Sophia, Em, and Sarah all sit on Jake and Sarah's front porch. Emmalynn spots me first, her face lighting up with that bright, toothy grin that never fails to make me smile.

"Daddy!" she squeals, scrambling off the porch and barreling towards me at full speed. I crouch down, bracing myself as her little body crashes into mine, her arms wrapping around my neck in a fierce hug. I scoop her up effortlessly, peppering her rosy cheeks with noisy kisses until she giggles uncontrollably.

"There's my favorite girl," I murmur, nuzzling my nose against hers. "Did you have a good day with Gram?" Emmalynn nods enthusiastically.

"Uh huh! Gram let me feed Barrett his bottle all by myself. I think he likes when I do it more than anyone else." A warm sense of pride blooms in my chest at her words.

"Is that so? I'm sure you're the very best bottle giver in the whole world then. I got something for you," I say, pulling the lightsaber I have tucked under my arm.

Emmalynn's eyes go wide as saucers when she spots the plastic toy, her little mouth dropping open in awe.

"Is that a real lightsaber, daddy?" she whispers, her voice filled with wonder. I can't help but smile at her innocence.

"It's as real as they come, baby girl. And it's all yours."

She reaches out with trembling hands, her fingers closing around it gently like it's the most precious thing in the world. In an instant, she's squirming out of my arms, her feet hitting the ground running as she takes off across the yard, swinging the lightsaber wildly and making swooshing noises.

"Fear me, evil Sith Lords!" she cries out, her voice carrying on the wind. "I am a Jedi Knight, protector of the galaxy!"

In moments like these, it's easy to forget about the darkness that constantly looms over our world. The club, the violence, the never-ending cycle of revenge and retribution. None of it matters when I see the pure, unbridled joy on my daughter's face. I make my way to the porch, giving Gram a kiss on the cheek.

"She's quite the little warrior, isn't she?" Gram muses. I nod, my eyes never leaving Emmalynn as she battles imaginary foes across the lawn.

"She's fearless. Just like her mama was."

Gram rests a comforting hand on my shoulder, giving it a gentle squeeze.

"Rebecca would be so proud of the way you're raising her, Rex. You're doing a damn fine job."

"I'm trying. Every single day, I'm tryin'. Thanks for watching my best girl today, Gram," I murmur, pulling her into a one-armed hug. She pats my cheek affectionately.

"You know I love having that sweet girl around. Wouldn't have it any other way." Turning to Sarah, I raise an inquisitive eyebrow.

"Where's Anna at?"

"Inside changing Barrett," she replies with a soft smile. "She said she was going to try rocking him and put him down for a nap after."

I give a slow nod, the corners of my mouth tugging upwards at the thought of Anna with my nephew. I push open the front door and step inside. The living room is quiet, save for the soft creak of the rocking chair coming from Barrett's room. Anna's eyes flicker up, meeting my gaze.

"Hey," I whisper. A gentle smile tugs at the corners of her mouth.

"Hey," she answers back as she nods towards the empty chair beside her. "He just dozed off," she murmurs, her voice barely above a whisper. "I didn't want to move him and risk waking him up."

I silently cross the room to sink into the chair next to her. Up close, I can see the dark smudges of exhaustion beneath her eyes, the lingering shadows of the torment she's endured. And yet, there's a peacefulness about her in this moment that I haven't witnessed before.

"I'm gonna grab one of Jake's beers and go sit on the back porch. You wanna come out when you're done with him?"

Anna's eyes light up a little at my question. "Yeah, I'll be right out."

I slip out of the room, letting Anna have her moment with Barrett. Making my way to the kitchen, I grab a couple of cold beers from the fridge before heading out the back door.

The evening sun casts a warm glow over the backyard. I settle into one of the weathered Adirondack chairs, cracking open a beer and taking a long pull. My eyes drift shut as I lean back, savoring the momentary peace and quiet.

It's not long before I hear the creak of the back door. I open my eyes to see Anna emerging, a small smile playing at her lips when she sees me. She sinks into the chair next to mine, accepting the beer I offer her.

We sit in comfortable silence for a few minutes, enjoying the warm breeze and the sounds of Emmalynn's giggles carrying over from the front yard.

"Gunnar and my dad wanted me to run something by you," I begin slowly. "They were really impressed with how much you helped out today, digging into the financials and all the intel you gave them."

Anna looks a little confused, but she gives me a nod to go on.

"They want to offer you a job with the club," I explain. "Working with Gunnar on the books for our various businesses and transport operations. He's got more work than he can handle alone these days."

Her eyes widen in surprise. "A job? With the club?"

I nod, watching her carefully. "It's just an offer, no pressure at all. But they think your skills would be a huge asset, and it would free up Gunnar to focus on other things."

Anna falls silent, chewing her lower lip as she mulls it over. Part of me worries it might be too much too soon for her. The last thing I want is to see her overextended and overwhelmed.

Finally, she meets my gaze, a determined glint in her eye. "I want to do it."

I can't help but smile at her fiery response. "You sure? We can take it slow if you need to ease into it."

But Anna is already shaking her head adamantly. "No, I don't want to go slow on this. I need to keep myself busy, keep my mind occupied. It's the only way I'll stay sane."

There's a haunted look that flashes across her face, and I know she's referring to the nightmares and panic attacks that still plague her. My chest tightens at the thought of her suffering alone with those demons.

Reaching out, I give her hand a reassuring squeeze. "Alright then. I'll let Gunnar know you're on board. We'll get you set up and he can start showing you the ropes."

Relief washes over Anna's features as she gives me a grateful smile. "Thank you, Rex. For everything."

Our eyes lock, and I feel that same magnetic pull towards her that I've been fighting for weeks now. She holds my gaze, almost challenging me to make a move.

But the moment is shattered by the sound of the back door swinging open. We both turn to see Jake emerging, a confused look on his face.

"You two just gonna sit out here and drink all my beer?"

"We were working on it."

Jake walks over handing me another beer. "Here you need it more than me. I'd be getting shitfaced too if I got my ass handed to me by some fuckin' dork swinging a glow stick and a prospect."

CHAPTER 8

Rex

We're all gathered in the chapel, the large wooden table filling the dimly lit room. On the screen before us, video feeds from the other nine Rebel Sons chapters flicker to life one by one.

My dad stands at the head of the table, his expression grim as he surveys the assembled leaders.

"Alright boys, listen up. We've been planning and preparing for this moment. In two weeks, we strike hard and fast."

Jax clicks a button and images, documents, and schematics pop up on the screen. It's everything we've been compiling on Moretti's operations over the past few months.

"Anna, Gunnar, and Jax have given us a detailed roadmap to bankrupt this bastard. We'll be hitting him from every angle... freezing accounts, seizing assets, dismantling his businesses piece by piece."

Beau gestures towards the West Coast team.

"Vincent Ruso has been sent to Portland by Moretti to oversee the organizations trafficking ring since we took Michael out a few months back. Jake, I want you to take the lead in eliminating this prick."

My muscles tense instinctively at the mention of the man who'd overseen Anna's captivity along with Michael. My dad must sense my reaction because he shoots me a pointed look before going on.

There's a rumble of approval, but then Anna's voice cuts through the noise, whispering so only I can hear.

"Just take him out?" There's an edge of bitterness I've never heard from her before. "A quick death is much more than he deserves after what he did to me."

I make a split-second decision. "Change of plans," I interject, rising from my seat. "I'll handle Vincent. Jake, you're leading the team to blow those shipping warehouses at the port where the girls are kept."

Jake looks like he's about to protest, but I silence him with a hard stare. My dad simply nods in approval.

I feel Anna's grateful gaze on me and give her the smallest of nods. She's been to hell and back, if anyone deserves vengeance, it's her.

"The rest of the orders stay the same," Beau continues. "We go in fast, we go in hard, and we cripple this whole damn operation in one coordinated strike. No mercy given."

A chorus of rumbling agreement echoes from the video feeds as the other chapters voice their readiness. I catch Jake's eye and he gives me an approving nod, understanding why I took this on myself.

"Listen up, this is how it's gonna go down," my dad continues, his voice carrying the weight of a man who's seen more than his fair share of bloodshed.

"Tacoma will be with North Ridge in Portland on strike day. Bishop and Canyon City, you're heading to LA to take care of Regali Imports. Vito Trinci runs that place."

“The walls in the basement are filled with cash. Take every single penny and then destroy the entire building. Leave nothing standing.”

"Consider it done, Beau," Ranger, the Canyon City President affirms. "My boys and Bishop have it handled."

Jax's fingers fly over the keys on his keyboard, no doubt arranging the necessary explosives for our mission.

"Trinidad and Reno, you're headed to Santoro Family Vineyards in Santa Rosa. Stephen Molinari is your target there. Anna says there's a vault in the wine cellar with logs detailing every transaction the Moretti's have made and with who. Open that son of a bitch up and take everything inside... cash, data, valuables, the whole nine yards. Now here's the kicker, Sledge" dad says, his gaze boring into the Reno Prez on the video feed.

"The vault opens with a fingerprint scanner. Specifically, it needs Stephen's right thumb to open. So... you got two choices. You grab the prick himself and make him open it..." A feral grin splits my dad's face. "Or just take the fuckers thumb and be done with it."

The head of the Trinidad crew, Wolf, chuckles darkly. "That prick won't be thumbing rides anymore."

"Rocky Mount and Hazard, I need a few of your men to go to Jersey, take out old man Moretti and the rest ride out to New York.

My heart rate kicks up a notch at the mention of Tony Moretti, the man responsible for the hell Anna's endured her entire life. Dealing with that scumbag myself would be deeply satisfying, but I know better than to question my President's orders. My dad continues, his voice like gravel.

"Crestview Construction & Development, Paulie Ciccio is your target. Take him out and blow the whole place sky-fucking-high. Make sure you destroy any machinery and equipment too. We don't want any civilian casualties though, so be careful."

I catch Anna's gaze, her expression unreadable. No tears, no fear, just that same cold determination I've seen flickering behind her eyes more and more lately.

"Strike Day will be in two weeks' time," dad says, his voice echoing through the chapel. "Jax will send each chapter the details on what business they're hitting and who needs to be dealt with."

"This all needs to be coordinated so it happens at the same time," his voice carrying an edge that demands absolute obedience. "We take out the entire organization at once. It's gotta be a surprise hit."

He turns his steely gaze towards the video feeds. "Get with the chapter you're working with and make a plan with Jax. He's researched every one of these businesses and locations, so he can tell you the best routes in. If any of you Texas boys in Dumas or Durango want to join the fun, you're more than welcome. Any questions?"

The room is deathly silent, every face a mask of grim focus.

"Good. Then I'll leave you boys to start preparing. We end this shit, once and for all, on our terms."

With that, Beau slams his fist on the table and the video feeds blink out one by one until only the core North Ridge members remain in the chapel. Anna hasn't moved a muscle, her gaze locked on the carved emblem in the center of the table.

"You know there's no going back after this," I murmur, drawing her eyes to meet mine. "Once we launch this offensive, it's all or nothing."

For a beat, she holds my stare, jaw set with grim determination. Then, giving the slightest of nods, she rises from her chair.

"I know. Let's burn it all to the ground."

CHAPTER 9

Anna

Gunnar walks me through the details of the job the club has offered me. As the club's treasurer, he spends hours with me examining ledgers, bank statements, and transaction records.

Gunnar patiently guided me through the financial records of each business the club owns, teaching me the subtle details and complexities of each.

The job would be demanding, but it gave me a sense of purpose and allowed me to focus my energy on something productive. With Gunnar's support and trust in me, I started to feel more sure of myself. I took pride in knowing I was making a valuable contribution to the club after everything they have done for me.

As we worked through each business, I gained a more comprehensive understanding of the club's financial landscape. It's an elaborate tangle of both legitimate and illicit activities that keeps the club's operations afloat. It's a mysterious world, where every move holds significance, and no detail can be overlooked.

I sat hunched over the desk in my office Gunnar put together for me. The dim glow of the desk lamp casting long shadows across the stacks of ledgers and files strewn before me. The familiar scent of motor oil and grease lingered in the air, a reminder that this makeshift office was in the back of the garage of the club's transport business on the compound.

It was late, but I wanted to go over the Moretti financials one more time to make sure there wasn't anything I missed with strike day approaching. Gunnar had trusted me with this task, and I was determined not to let him or the Rebel Sons down.

I meticulously scanned each page, carefully comparing every transaction, account balance, and questionable discrepancy. The Moretti family's network of unlawful transactions was complex and confusing, but I was determined to untangle it.

All of a sudden, I noticed a pattern that had escaped my attention before. The Moretti family was making payments to the Garza Cartel that were much larger than the agreed-upon amounts for the drugs they were receiving in return. It didn't make sense.

I leaned back in my seat, deep in thought. Was it possible that Michael was stealing money from the cartel? The consequences would be massive.

Feeling determined, I delved further into the records, following the money trails and uncovering even more proof of Michael's deceit. The figures were crystal clear; he had been taking a cut for himself, stealing from the cartel.

My heart raced as I realized the gravity of this discovery. Not only had Michael betrayed the cartel, but he had also been siphoning funds from his own organization, weakening its financial foundations. This information could prove invaluable to the Rebel Sons.

I quickly gathered the relevant documents and hurried out of my office, determined to share my findings with Gunnar and the rest of the club.

Leaving my office, I hurried through the dimly lit garage, clutching the stack of documents in my hands. I spotted Rex hunched over a workbench, tinkering with the go-kart for Emmalynn.

"Rex," I called out, drawing his attention.

He straightened up, wiping the grease from his hands with a rag.

"Anna, what's going on?"

"I've been going over the Moretti financials again, and I think I've found something." I quickly explained my discovery about Michael's embezzlement from the Garza Cartel. Rex's eyes widened as he listened, a low whistle escaping his lips.

"Damn, that's big. Good catch, sweetheart." He took the documents from my hands, scanning them intently.

"Gunnar needs to see this."

Rex nodded, a small smile tugging at the corners of his mouth. "You've been doing one hell of a job, Anna. Gunnar's been singing your praises, and the club's real impressed with how you've been helping us."

I felt a surge of pride at his words, but also a twinge of unease. "I just want to make sure I'm doing everything I can to help. After what they've done to me, my mom, and Sarah, I want to see them pay."

Rex placed a gentle hand on my shoulder, his touch sending a shiver down my spine. "I know, and you've been invaluable. Dad and the others are real grateful. You're making a difference, Anna."

His words of encouragement and the warmth in his gaze made me feel seen and understood in a way I hadn't experienced in a long time.

"I have to head to Portland in a few days to watch Vincent Russo and learn his daily routine," he explained, his brows knitting together in deep thought. "I need to figure out the best time to take him out."

My heart raced at the mention of Vincent. The thought of Rex putting himself in harm's way to protect me sent a wave of anxiety through me.

"What about Emmalynn?" I asked, the worry evident in my voice. "Who's going to look after her while you're gone?"

Rex placed a gentle hand on my arm, his touch instantly calming my nerves. "Actually, I wanted to talk to you about that, Anna. I was hoping you and Sarah could help Gram keep an eye on Em while I'm away."

"Of course, I'd be happy to help," I assured him.

Rex's eyes met mine, his gaze filled with a warmth that made my heart flutter. "I appreciate that. And I wanted to make sure you'll be okay while I'm gone. You can call or text me anytime, you hear? I'll be just a phone call away."

His words soothed the lingering anxiety within me. The thought of having Rex's unwavering support, even from a distance, was a comfort I hadn't realized I needed so desperately.

"I'll be fine, Rex," I replied, offering him a small smile. "I know you and the others will be taking care of business. Just promise me you'll be careful, okay?"

I knew the danger he was about to face, but I also knew that he was a force to be reckoned with.

Rex chuckled, the deep rumble of his voice sending a shiver down my spine. "You got it. I'll be back before you know it."

Rex's warm gaze held mine, his stare causing my heart to race. Slowly, he reached up and cupped my cheek, his calloused fingers sending tingles across my skin.

"I'm gonna miss you while I'm gone," he murmured, his voice low and gruff.

I was unable to react before his lips were already pressed against mine, the kiss intense and full of desire. My eyes shut as I lost myself in the warmth of his embrace, all worries about the risks he would be taking vanishing. For those few seconds, it was just him and I, wrapped up in our own little universe.

Rex pulled away, his breathing ragged. "Finish up in the office, sweetheart," he said, his thumb caressing my cheek. "I'll walk you back to the townhouses."

I gave a small nod, still dazed from the feeling of his lips on mine. As he turned to head back to his work, I couldn't help but admire the way his muscles moved beneath his shirt.

Gathering the documents I wanted to show Gunnar, I followed Rex out of the garage, my hand shaking slightly in his. The walk back to the townhouses was quiet, but the air was thick with unspoken emotions.

As we reached my door, Rex pulled me into his arms, his lips brushing against my forehead. "Get some rest, alright?"

I watched him as he strode down the steps of the porch, his strong shoulders and confident stride a reassuring sight. Sighing, I went inside and made my way up to my room.

Closing the door behind me, I leaned back against it, my fingers tracing my lips where Rex's had been. The warmth of his touch lingered, a silent promise that he would return to me. With a deep breath, I crossed the room and sank down onto my bed.

Lying there, I can still taste Rex's lips on mine. My hand trembles as I trace it along my own skin, pretending it's his rough, calloused touch. The intensity in his gaze had stirred something inside of me that I thought was long gone after everything

Michael and his crew inflicted on me in that dark basement.

Recently, I found myself daydreaming about Rex's touch more and more, often tracing the faint scars on my wrists with my fingertips while Rex's voice echoed in my mind, 'You're safe with me, sweetheart.'

Tentatively, I slid a shaking hand under my sleep shorts, pretending it was Rex's gentle touch on my tender flesh. I close my eyes, trying to block out the memories of the cruelty that had last touched my body. Instead, I focused on Rex. His eyes, so blue and penetrating, held a promise of safety and protection that I hadn't known existed before him.

As my fingers danced across my skin, a wave of intense pleasure washed over me. The mere thought of Rex sent electric currents through my body, igniting a fiery passion within me. I closed my eyes and let myself drown in the ecstasy, pushing away any thoughts other than those of Rex and the pleasure he could give me.

As I gently stroked my clit, I could feel my mind drifting away from the painful memories of my past. My body relaxed into the fantasy of being nurtured and cherished. A soft sigh escapes my lips as I close my eyes and allow my mind to wander. Images of Rex's touch, his warm kisses on my lips, and his hands exploring every inch of my body flood my thoughts, leaving me with an intense ache of desire.

As I close my eyes, Rex's face floats in my mind, a gentle smile gracing his lips as he traces a line of kisses along my neck and chest.

"That's it, baby," he whispered in my ear. "Let me make you feel good."

The sensations consumed me, my breathing becoming ragged as I surrendered to the pleasure. My fingers delved between my thighs, slick with desire as I traced them along my throbbing clit. My moans grew louder as I got lost in the fantasy of Rex's touch, I moaned and writhed, my body aching for release that only he could give.

I ground my hips against my hand, fantasizing about him buried deep inside me. With each thrust, my moans grew louder. My fingers dug into the sheets and my body trembled with pleasure. As my climax built, I let out a moan, biting my lip to muffle the sound. I couldn't hold back any longer.

My body arched as I called out Rex's name, the sound echoing in my ears as pure ecstasy coursed through me. It was a moment of raw, unadulterated passion and all I wanted was more. I wanted more of him.

I lay there, my heart pounding in my chest, I couldn't help but wonder if Rex, could ever feel the same way about me, if he knew what had been done to me.

He was a man of depth, his past as murky and mysterious as the black ink adorning his skin. Yet, I knew he held an unwavering loyalty and a tender heart for those close to him. I yearned to be one of those people, to experience the intensity of our make-believe connection in reality, to feel the heat of our bodies entwined, and to be consumed by the passion that flowed through my veins.

I wanted to know what it meant to be claimed by Rex Riggs.

CHAPTER 10

Rex

After I kissed Anna, I walked her back to her place. Now, lying in bed, I can't help but feel like an asshole. It was an impulsive move on my part; I should have known she wasn't ready for that yet.

Just then, through the thin wall separating our rooms, I froze as I heard the unmistakable sounds coming from the other side. I couldn't resist listening in. With each moan and gasp, my curiosity turned to excitement as I thought about what she was doing on the other side of the wall. My imagination ran wild with images of Anna getting herself off. Those sexy as fuck moans from her mouth were a far cry from the timid girl I first met.

As I lay there listening, my body responded to the sounds coming from the other side of the wall. My cock was so fucking hard. I could hear the bedsprings creak wildly beneath her and imagined her lying there writhing with pleasure. My hand instinctively reached down palming my dick, trying to get control of myself.

Her moans were getting louder, I couldn't take it anymore. Freeing myself, my hand griped my thick, pulsating cock, roughly. The skin sliding up and down with each stroke, pumping faster to match Anna's rhythm. Veins bulge and pulse beneath my hand, evidence of my arousal.

With my eyes closed, I could see Anna's face. The way her soft, porcelain skin would glow in the dim light of the room. I can see her lips parting and her body moving, her slick pussy grinding against her hand with each stroke.

My mouth waters with the thought of tasting her. I imagine the salty sweetness of her skin and the taste of her arousal. The thought drives me wild, and I picture my tongue tracing every inch of her body as I continue stroking myself.

I'm so turned on listening to the sexy as fuck sounds Anna is making. My imagination runs wild with thoughts of how she would writhe and moan beneath me. My cock is throbbing, and my hand moves faster and harder against its length. With my eyes closed, I could almost feel her body pressed against mine. Her skin, soft and warm against my rough hands.

And then I hear it... her orgasm hit and she cried out my name as she came.

My eyes flew open as I lost all control. My body trembled as a powerful orgasm ripped through me, my mind consumed with thoughts of her. She came thinking of me, with my name on her lips.

* * *

I drag my ass out of bed, feeling a mixture of arousal and guilt about last night. As much as I want Anna, I know she's been through hell. I question if I'm the man she truly needs. I care for Anna, but I don't know if I'm the man she needs or deserves. Do I even want to be? Settling down again was never part of the plan. I know for damn sure I don't want any other man taking that place in her life. I grab a t-shirt and jeans before heading down the hall to Emmalynn's room.

"C'mon baby girl, time to get ready for school." Her little face lights up when she sees me.

"Morning daddy!" She leaps into my arms, still in her princess pajamas.

After getting her dressed and fed, we head out to the truck. On the drive, I dread having to tell her I'll be gone for a week.

"Hey Em, I have to go out of town for a few days to work."

Her smile fades. "How long?"

"Just for a week, baby. I'll be back before you know it." I ruffle her curly hair, so much like her mother's. When we pull up to the school, she looks up at me with those big eyes.

"Is Grandpa gonna do pizza night with me while you're gone?" Shit. I forgot all about it.

"No, honey, Grandpa has to leave for a few days too for the club." Her little lip trembles and I feel like a piece of shit father. But then her face brightens.

"Can Anna do pizza night?" I pause, picturing Anna covered in flour, laughing with Emmalynn. A small smile plays across my lips.

"I'll stop and ask Anna before I leave if she can. If not, I'll ask Gram and Sarah. I'm sure they would love to do pizza night with you." Emmalynn throws her little arms around my neck.

"I love you, daddy."

"Love you too, princess." I hug her tight before letting her jump out of the truck. As I watch her run towards the school, I realize just how much Anna has become a part of not just my life but Em's too.

I return to the compound, my thoughts wrapped up in my upcoming job. I acknowledge the prospects on guard duty before entering.

The main room is a chaotic scene, with members crowded around the pool tables and bar. I spot Jake in the corner, going over some gear laid out on the table.

"Rex," he calls out, waving me over. "Got your care package ready to go for your trip." I eye the backpack and cases, mentally checking off the contents.

"Anything I need to know?"

Jake shakes his head. "Nah, standard issue. Couple of backup pieces, ammo, some small explosives, detonators. Enough toys to make Vincent's last few moments memorable for both of you."

A twisted grin spreads across my face. "Can't wait, it's gonna be a hell of a party."

After getting the rundown from Jake, I make my way towards the garage to find Anna. Her office door is ajar, and I can hear her rapid typing as I approach. I rap my knuckles lightly against the doorframe.

Anna looks up, her eyes meeting mine. "Hey," she says softly, a slight flush coloring her cheeks.

"Hey yourself." I lean against the doorframe, taking in the sight of her. "I'm heading out in a bit. Wanted to check in before I go."

She rises from her chair, crossing the small space to stand before me. Up close, I can see the dark circles of exhaustion beneath her eyes.

"Be careful out there, okay?" Her concern for me catches me off guard.

I nod, "always am."

Anna worries her lower lip between her teeth, and I have to resist the urge to pull her into my arms. "I'll keep an eye on Emmalynn while you're gone. Don't worry about her."

"I know you will. Friday night. Would you mind doing pizza

night with Em?" I scratch the back of my neck. "She got a little upset this morning when I told her I'd be out of town. She asked if you could do it with her."

A soft smile spreads across her lips. "Of course, I'd love to."

"I always leave some cash in the jar on the kitchen counter. You two can get whatever you want. Just send Park to the store with a list of what you need. Thanks sweetheart, I appreciate it."

I turn to leave her office but pause in the doorway, glancing over my shoulder into the garage bays to ensure we're alone. Lowering my voice, I take a step back towards her.

"Oh, Anna? Next time you want me to make you come, just ask baby. I'll show you what the real thing is like. I promise it'll be a hell of a lot better than what you can imagine, and more satisfying than your own hand."

With a wink, I spin on my heel and stride out, leaving Anna flustered and flushed. This trip to Portland can't be over soon enough.

I swing my leg over my bike, the engine rumbling to life beneath me. Gripping the throttle, I peel out of the compound, leaving a cloud of dust in my wake. The open road stretches before me, but my mind is focused on one thing, Vincent Ruso.

That sick bastard laid his hands on something that didn't belong to him. Someone good and innocent who had already been through enough suffering. The thought of what Anna endured twists my gut into knots.

As the miles fly by, the scenery around me passes in a blur. I grip the handlebars tightly, my knuckles turning white. Ruso's face is seared into my mind. That smug smile and those cold, dead eyes. He's a poison that needs to be eradicated.

I picture Anna's face, her haunted gaze when I carried her out of that basement. The bruises, the fear etched into her delicate features. She didn't deserve that hell. No one does. But I'll be damned if I let another monster lay a hand on her again.

My rage builds with every twist of the road. Flashes of her soft skin, her gentle smiles meant only for me, fuel the fire in my veins. She's a light in the darkness, and I'll burn this fucking world down to keep her that way.

After hours on the road, Portland's city limits finally come into view. I downshift, the growl of my bike's engine echoing through the streets as I close in on my target's location. Time to get to work.

I slip into the shadows, blending into the darkness. I watch Ruso's every move from a distance. He carries himself with an air of superiority, as if he is the ruler of this city. Little does he know the punishment that awaits.

I will bide my time, and when the moment is right, I'll strike. No one touches what's mine and lives to tell about it. Anna is under my protection now. Anyone who dares to challenge that better start praying to whatever god they believe in, because in my eyes, they are already dead.

CHAPTER 11

Rex

I arrived in Portland one week prior to the planned strike, my sole purpose to prepare for one task: eliminating Vincent Ruso. The mere thought of his touch on her skin made my blood boil with rage. He was the only remaining piece of trash who hurt her that needed to be taken care of.

I settle into the plain, nondescript motel room on the outskirts of Portland. Methodically, I unpack my duffel, laying out the tools of my trade. Surveillance equipment, maps of the city, and a small arsenal that would make any self-respecting gun enthusiast drool.

Pinning a map of Portland to the wall, I mark Ruso's known haunts and the Moretti family's business fronts with red pushpins. My eyes narrow as I study the landscape, visualizing the bastard's daily movements. Ruso may think he's untouchable, but he's about to learn that the Rebel Sons have a long reach and an even longer memory.

I set up a makeshift command center on the rickety table, arranging my laptop and police scanner. Hacking into the city's CCTV network is child's play with the skills Jax taught me. Soon, I have eyes on every street corner and alleyway in Ruso's territory.

As I clean my guns, my mind drifts to Anna. The thought of her delicate frame battered and bruised ignites a fury in my veins. I picture her soft smile, the way her eyes light up when she laughs at Emmalynn's antics. The need to protect her, to make those who hurt her pay, consumes me.

I clear my head and focus on the mission at hand. Emotions won't help in this situation. I'm here to do a job, to eliminate a threat to my club and the woman who's come to mean more to me than I care to admit.

As the sky turns orange, the city skyline is bathed in the warm glow of sunset. I crack my knuckles and get to work. Vincent Ruso may be a ghost to everyone else, but I'm the fucking grim reaper and he's the next name on my list.

The following day, I find a comfortable spot in the corner of a coffee shop, my gaze fixated on the towering building just across the street. This is where Vincent Ruso resides, in a luxurious penthouse apartment on the top floor.

As I sip on my strong black coffee, I take in the constant stream of activity around the building. My mind takes note of every detail. From the security guards stationed at the entrance to the expensive cars that transport Ruso's associates back and forth.

Right on cue, Ruso emerges from the building, his expensive suit crisp and his step brisk. I watch as he strides to a waiting SUV, his security detail falling into place around him. The vehicle pulls away, and I quickly toss a few bills on the table before heading out to follow.

The drive takes us to an upscale gym, where Ruso disappears inside, his bodyguards taking up positions around the entrance. I park a few blocks down, blending into the flow of pedestrian traffic as I make my way closer.

Ruso emerges an hour later, his face flushed from his workout. He pauses to chat with a few well-dressed individuals before climbing back into his SUV. As the day wears on, I continue my surveillance, cataloging Ruso's movements and habits. He's a creature of habit, his schedule as predictable as the ticking of a clock.

The sun dips below the horizon, casting long shadows across the city streets. I stretch my stiff muscles, my eyes never leaving the high-rise. Ruso's silhouette appears in the window, a glass of amber liquid in his hand as he gazes out at the city. I can practically feel the self-satisfaction rolling off him in waves.

Soon, that arrogance will be wiped from his face. I'm going to make him pay for what he's done, for the pain he's caused. And I'll do it with my own two hands.

I spent three days straight observing Ruso's movements, studying his patterns like a hunter stalking its prey. The more I learned about this dick bag, the more my disgust for him grew.

On the third night, I followed Ruso to the same high-end gentlemen's club he has come to every night, the Black Lotus. It's the kind of place that caters to the whims of the rich and powerful.

What is unexpected, is that he only brings one bodyguard with him when he comes to this club. Everywhere else he goes he is accompanied by at least three bodyguards.

I slipped through the door behind them, the pulsing music and dim lighting providing ample cover. Taking a seat at the back corner of the bar, I ordered a whiskey and settled in to watch.

My eyes swept over the club, noting the entrances, exits, and the positions of security cameras and personnel. I'd have to be careful when making my move, leave no room for error.

As I sipped my drink, I watched Ruso work the room, schmoozing with the other patrons like a master manipulator. He oozed confidence, as if he owned the place and everyone in it.

Every night, Ruso would beckon one particular girl over, his hand possessively gripping her arm as he led her towards the private rooms in the back. Tonight was no different.

I signaled the bartender, a weathered man with a tired gaze. "Who's the girl Ruso took back there?" He glanced over his shoulder before leaning in close.

"That's Velvet. Been working here a few months now."

My phone vibrates in my pocket. Taking it out I see it's a text from X.

X: At the motel. In the room beside you on the corner.

Me: There in 20

* * *

"Listen up," I growl, my voice low and gritty as Dom and X settle into the chairs across from me. "We only got one shot at this, so pay attention." I tap the map spread out on the table, the red pushpins marking Ruso's movements like a twisted game of connect-the-dots.

"For the past three days, I've been tailing that piece of shit, learning his routine inside and out."

Dom leans forward, his eyes intent. "What've you got for us, Rex?"

Jabbing a finger at the map, I lay it all out. "He starts his day at the gym, gets his workout in before hitting up whatever business he's got cookin' that day. Evenings, he heads to the same strip club every night, only takes one guard with him." X raises an eyebrow, his expression pensive.

"Interesting. He lettin' his guard down?" I shake my head, the hard line of my jaw tightening.

"Nah, the prick's arrogant as hell. Thinks he's untouchable in that place. Spends his nights getting lap dances and taking girls to the private rooms."

Disgust twists my gut as I recall the scene from last night. Ruso, his hands all over some poor girl, treating her like she was nothing more than a possession to be used.

"Way I see it, we got two options. We can hit him at the club, take him out while he's feeling nice and comfortable. Or we trail him after, grab him when he's alone."

X drums his fingers on the table, mulling over the choices. "Club could be risky, lots of civilians in the crossfire. But if we wait till after, he might not be as isolated as we'd like."

"Which is why," I interject, "I say we go with option one. We do it at the club. Catch him while he's only got one guard."

Leaning back in my chair, I run a hand through my hair.

"Here's how it's gonna go down. We'll hit Ruso at the club, he takes the same girl into the same private room every night. I'll kill the fucker in that room. We catch the bastard with his pants down... literally and figuratively."

As I lay it all out for Dom and X, I can feel the adrenaline already pumping through my veins.

"We're gonna need to move fast and hit him hard. No room for mistakes."

X nods, his jaw set in a hard line. He's been itching for a piece of this action ever since we found out Ruso was one of the men who hurt Anna. Ruso also helped Michael Moretti organize the kidnapping of Jake's old lady, Sarah, their son Barrett, and Jake's sister Cassandra. X thinks he hides his feelings for Cass, but everyone knows he's got it bad for her.

Turning my attention to Dom, "you're goin' in the front of the club, kid. Keep an eye on Ruso, when he calls the girl over to go into the private room, you text X and let us know it's go time.

Then you're gonna need to start a fight and cause a pretty big scene. That way all the bouncers make their way to the front of the club. After you get thrown out, you set up across the street, keep an eye on any potential threats coming our way. If shit hits the fan, you text X and then provide cover."

I level my gaze on Dom, looking directly into his eyes. "Kid, I need you to really fucking hear me on this last part." Dom nods, and I know I have his full attention.

"DO… NOT… FUCKING… SHOOT… ME… Got it?"

Dom straightens in his seat, his expression serious. "You got it, Rex. I won't fucking shoot you."

"X, you're exiting the building first when we leave."

"What the fuck Rex?" X spits, half amused and half pissed.

"He's already tased me once and I have a kid at home. He can shoot you this time."

CHAPTER 12

Anna

I sit on the front porch, legs crossed, my fingers drumming against the wooden armrest of the rocking chair. The warm afternoon sun bathes the porch in a warm glow, and I squint against the bright rays. A gentle breeze ruffles the trees lining the driveway, and I take a deep breath, savoring the crisp mountain air.

In the distance, I hear the rumble of an approaching engine. A few moments later, Parker's truck comes into view, and I can make out the small figure of Emmalynn bouncing excitedly in the passenger seat.

As the truck pulls up, Emmalynn bursts out of the door as soon as Parker kills the engine, her backpack bouncing against her back as she races towards me.

"Anna!" she squeals, launching herself into my arms. I catch her with a laugh, hugging her tightly.

"Hey there, pretty girl. Did you have a good day at school?"

Emmalynn nods enthusiastically, her dark curls bobbing.

"The best! We got to play outside for extra recess, and it was my turn today for show and tell. I showed everyone the lightsaber daddy got me. I was green today! Green means I was good all day."

"That's amazing!" I praise, giving her another squeeze.

Parker approaches, a warm smile on his face.

"Hey, Anna. Here's the stuff from the grocery store you wanted. I'll be out front watching the gate. Just call if you need anything."

"Thank you, Park. I'll send some pizza out when it's done." I reply, setting Emmalynn down. "We're going to have a blast, aren't we, Em?" Emmalynn grins up at me, her eyes shining with excitement.

"Pizza night with the girls!"

Parker chuckles, ruffling her hair. "Alright, kiddo. You be good for Anna and the others, okay?"

"I will, Park," Emmalynn promises, already tugging on my hand. "Come on, Anna! Let's go get everything ready!"

I laugh and let her lead me inside, waving goodbye to Parker over my shoulder. As we enter the kitchen, I see that Marlene, Sarah, Cassandra, and my mom have already begun setting out the ingredients and utensils for our pizza-making extravaganza.

"There's my favorite little chef!" Marlene exclaims, enveloping Emmalynn in a warm hug.

Emmalynn giggles, her infectious joy filling the room. "Hi Gram! Hi Sarah! Hi Cassie! Hi Sophia!"

The women greet her with equal enthusiasm, and I can't help but smile at the scene before me. This is what family looks like, I realize. A sense of belonging washes over me.

As we begin to prepare the dough and toppings, laughter and chatter fill the air. Emmalynn takes charge, directing us with the confidence of a seasoned chef, and I find myself caught up in the pure joy of the moment.

This is what I've been missing, I think to myself. This is what it means to be part of something bigger than yourself, to be surrounded by love and acceptance. And as I catch Marlene's warm gaze, I know that I've finally found my place in the world.

"Hey Anna, can we have a sleepover too since daddy is gone? You can spend the night with me, and can you paint my fingernails? Do you have fingernail polish? Daddy won't let me have any because he thinks I'll make a mess," Emmalynn asks, her eyes wide and hopeful.

I can't resist her pleading gaze, and a warm smile spreads across my face.

"How about we call your dad and ask if that's okay? If he says it's okay, then we absolutely can have a sleepover, and then Gram can take the night off."

Emmalynn's face lights up with pure joy. "Yay! Can we call daddy now?"

I nod, reaching for my phone. "Of course, sweetie. Let's give him a call."

As I dial Rex's number, Emmalynn bounces on her toes with anticipation. The phone rings a few times before Rex's gruff voice answers.

"Hey, it's me," I say, my heart fluttering at the sound of his voice. "Emmalynn has a very important question to ask you." I hand the phone to Emmalynn, who takes it eagerly.

"Daddy? Can Anna and I have a sleepover tonight? And can she paint my nails too? Please, please, please?"

There's a pause as Rex considers her request, and I hold my breath, hoping he'll say yes. Emmalynn's eyes are wide and imploring, and I find myself silently pleading alongside her. Finally, Rex's voice comes through the speaker.

"Alright, princess. You can have a sleepover with Anna, but you have to promise to be a good girl and listen to her, okay?"

Emmalynn nods vigorously, even though he can't see her. "I promise, daddy! Thank you, thank you!"

I can't help but grin at her enthusiasm, as Emmalynn hands me back the phone. I take the phone from Emmalynn's outstretched hand, my heart fluttering.

"Hey, it's me again," I say, trying to keep my voice casual. There's a brief pause on the other end before Rex speaks.

"Hey. Everything going okay over there?"

"Yeah, everything's great," I assure him. "We're just getting started on the pizza-making. Emmalynn's already taken charge."

Rex chuckles, "that's my girl. Listen, Anna, I wanted to..." He trails off, and I can picture him running a hand over his face.

"What is it, Rex?" I prompt gently.

He exhales slowly. "Just have a good night. Don't hesitate to call me if you need anything. Anything at all."

His words are laced with a protective intensity that both comforts and thrills me. "I will. Don't worry about us. We're good here."

"I know," he says, his voice softening. "I trust you."

Those three simple words hit me like a punch to the gut, stealing my breath away. To have earned Rex's trust after everything I've been through... it means more than he could ever know.

"Thank you," I manage to whisper, blinking back the sudden moisture in my eyes.

There's another pause, and I can sense Rex's hesitation, as if he wants to say more but isn't sure how. Finally, he clears his throat.

"Alright, well, I should let you get back to it. Tell Emmalynn I love her, and I'll see you both soon."

As Rex and I say our goodbyes, I turn back to Emmalynn, who's practically vibrating with excitement.

"Alright, pretty girl, it looks like we're having a sleepover tonight!"

Emmalynn lets out a squeal of delight, throwing her arms around my waist. "This is going to be the best night ever!"

I laugh, hugging her back. "It sure is, Em. Now, let's finish making these pizzas so we can start our girls' night."

We return to the kitchen, where the others are waiting with knowing smiles. "So, I take it the sleepover is a go?" Marlene asks, her eyes twinkling.

I nod, grinning. "Looks like it's just us tonight, Gram. I hope you don't mind me stealing your granddaughter for the evening."

Marlene waves her hand dismissively. "Oh, don't you worry about that, dear. You two have a wonderful time. It's been a while since I've had a night to myself anyway."

* * *

Four hours later after the pizza has been made and we watched the movie Em picked out, I send Emmalynn upstairs to brush her teeth and get changed for bed. As soon as her little feet patter up the steps, the other women turn to me with curious expressions.

"Alright, spill it," Cassandra says, leaning forward. "What's really going on with the guys going to Portland?"

I glance around the kitchen, making sure Emmalynn is out of earshot before responding.

"They're working on a plan to take down the Moretti organization and their trafficking ring."

Gasps echo around the room, and Sarah nods grimly.

"Jake's been tense these past few days, preparing for this mission. I can only imagine how dangerous it must be."

"Beau called me earlier when he arrived in Portland," my mom, Sophia, adds. "He sounded more stressed than I've ever heard him in all the years I've been working for him and the club at the Ridge."

A heavy silence falls over the kitchen as we all process the gravity of the situation. These men, our loved ones, are willingly putting themselves in harm's way to dismantle a criminal empire.

"Do you know any details about their plan?" Marlene asks, her face etched with concern.

I shake my head. "Not really. Rex has been tight-lipped about it, for obvious reasons. All I know is that it's a coordinated strike, involving multiple chapters."

"God, I hope they know what they're doing," Cassandra mutters, chewing her lip anxiously.

Reaching across the table, I give her hand a reassuring squeeze.

"If anyone can pull this off, it's them. We just have to have faith and stay strong for when they return."

The women nod, their expressions a mix of worry and determination. We may not be on the frontlines, but our role is just as crucial. We have to hold down the fort and provide unwavering support for our men.

As if sensing the somber mood, Emmalynn bounds back into the kitchen, her hair damp and her pajamas adorned with little purple unicorns. "I'm ready for our sleepover!" she announces, beaming.

Her infectious joy is a much-needed reprieve, and we all can't help but smile at her enthusiasm. Tonight, we'll focus on creating happy memories, pushing aside our fears and worries until tomorrow.

"Well, in that case, how about we get started on those nails?" I suggest.

Her eyes light up, and she nods vigorously, hopping onto the chair beside me. As I pull out an array of nail polish colors, the other women gather around, offering suggestions and sharing stories.

For now, we'll revel in this moment of sisterhood and solidarity, drawing strength from one another. Because when our men return, they'll need us to be the rock they can lean on, the safe haven they can come home to.

And we'll be ready.

CHAPTER 13

Rex

I sit on my bike in the dimly lit employee parking lot behind the Black Lotus, keeping a watchful eye on the surroundings. X moves stealthily around the perimeter, testing the security system just as Jax had instructed. My grip tightens on the handlebars as I watch him work, the weight of tomorrow's mission weighing down heavily on me.

X gives me a thumbs up, signaling the all-clear. Our tech is good to bypass their system and kill the security feed when the time comes. A small victory, but a crucial one. I nod back, a silent acknowledgment passing between us.

Killing the engine, I dismount and make my way over to X. We go over the plan one more time, ensuring every detail is committed to memory. There's no room for error, not when so much is at stake.

"You good with your part?" I ask, my voice low.

X nods, his expression steely. "Locked and loaded."

I return to my motorcycle and wait, firing off a message to Jax. I'm hoping he can get ahold of the building schematics for me, allowing me to confirm I didn't overlook any additional rooms or exits. As I wrap up my exchange with Jax, Anna's name flashes on my screen with a new text. I open the message as soon as it appears.

Anna: Hey, are you busy? There someone here that really wants to tell you goodnight.

I call her right away.

"Hey sweetheart," I say as soon as Anna picks up. "Everything alright?"

There's a brief pause before she responds.

"Yeah, everything's fine. Everyone just left so we were just getting ready for bed."

"That's great, I'm real glad you had some company tonight," I tell her sincerely. "But you said someone wanted to say goodnight?"

There's a bit of shuffling on the other end before a tiny voice pipes up.

"Hi daddy!" My chest constricts at the sweet sound of Emmalynn's voice.

"Hey there, princess. You being a good girl for Anna and the ladies?"

"Uh huh!" she chirps. "And guess what daddy? The next sleepover we are gonna do makeovers! Anna said we can if you say it's okay."

I chuckle softly, picturing my little girl all dolled up. As much as I hate being away from her, I know Anna will take good care of her.

"You got my permission, baby. Just don't go giving Anna too hard of a time, alright?"

"I won't, I promise!" Her sweet giggle fills my ear.

I talk to Emmalynn for a little while longer, feeling a tinge of guilt for having this sweet conversation with my five-year-old daughter while standing outside a seedy strip club. But hearing her cheerful voice is like a ray of light piercing through the darkness of my current surroundings.

"Alright princess, it's getting late. You need to get some sleep," I tell her. "Can you put Anna back on for me?"

"Okay, night night, daddy. I love you!"

"Love you too, Em. Sweet dreams."

There's a bit of rustling as the phone gets passed over.

"Hey," Anna's voice comes through the speaker.

"Hey. Sorry about that, I know it's getting late." I look at the time on my phone. It's a little after midnight.

"No, don't worry about it. I'm glad Em got to talk to you."

I glance over at X who is leaning against the building, taking a smoke break.

"Listen, there's something I wanted to ask you about. I'm not really in a spot I can talk right now. It's going to be late when I get back to the motel tonight."

"Okay..." Anna replies hesitantly. "What is it?"

I pause, not wanting to go into details standing in this parking lot with X.

"I'd rather explain it later. Would you mind if I call you later? Even if it's the middle of the night?"

"Yeah, just call whenever you can."

"Okay, I'll call you as soon as I can. Get some sleep Anna."

"Night Rex."

Hitting end, I slip the phone back into my pocket, my mind refocusing on the task at hand. I glance over at X, who's reviewing the schematics Jax just sent over.

"Anything we missed?" I ask, peering at the blueprints over his shoulder.

"Nah, man. We got everything covered. Once we talk to this chick," X nods towards the back of the strip club. "Then we got everything in place, and we are good to go."

We stood there waiting for another two and a half hours before Velvet walked out the back of the club heading towards the employee parking lot. She freezes mid-step when she sees us and realizes she isn't alone. A panicked look on her face.

I hold my hands up in front of me. "Whoa Darlin', don't worry. We just want to talk to you for a minute. Actually, I need to ask you a favor."

I approach Velvet slowly, keeping my hands visible to show I mean no harm. The poor girl looks like a deer caught in headlights, her eyes wide with fear.

"Listen, Velvet," I begin, my voice low and calm. "I got a proposition for you. A way for you to make some easy cash."

She eyes me warily, her body tense. "What kind of proposition?"

I glance around to make sure no one else is within earshot before continuing. "Tomorrow night, when Ruso takes you into that private room, I need you to leave the door unlocked. Someone's gonna come in after you two."

Velvet's eyes widen even further, her face paling.

"I-I can't do that. Ruso... he'll kill me if he finds out."

I shake my head. "He won't find out. All you gotta do is keep your mouth shut and walk out of the room as soon as the other person enters. You do that, and I'll hand you five grand. Cash."

She stares at me, her jaw slack.

"Five thousand dollars? Just for leaving a door unlocked?"

"That's right. Five grand, and all you gotta do is walk away and forget this conversation ever happened."

Velvet chews on her bottom lip, clearly torn. I can practically see the gears turning in her head as she weighs the risks against the tempting payout.

"How do I know this isn't some kind of setup?" she asks, her voice trembling slightly.

I meet her gaze steadily. "Because if I wanted to set you up, I wouldn't be standing here offering you money. I'd just do what I needed to do and leave you to deal with the fallout."

She considers this for a long moment before finally nodding.

"Okay. I'll do it. But I want half the money up front. Tonight."

I nod, reaching into my pocket and pulling out a wad of cash. I count out twenty-five hundred dollars and hold it out to her.

"Half now, half tomorrow after you walk out of that room. We got a deal?"

Velvet takes the money with shaking hands, stuffing it into her purse. "Deal."

"Good. Remember, just leave the door unlocked and walk away. Nothing else."

She nods, her face pale but determined. I watch as she hurries to her car, casting nervous glances over her shoulder.

I turn to X, who's been standing silently beside me the whole time. "Let's go."

I'm back at the motel, my body heavy with exhaustion. The adrenaline from earlier has long since faded, leaving me feeling drained. I strip off my clothes and step into the shower, letting the hot water cascade over my tense muscles.

As I stand under the spray, my mind replays the events of the night. The plan is in motion, the pieces falling into place. But the weight of what's to come still sits heavy on my shoulders.

I finish my shower and towel off, slipping into a pair of boxers. I stretch out on the bed, the cool sheets a welcome relief against my skin. I reach for my phone on the nightstand, my fingers hovering over Anna's contact.

I hesitate for a moment, glancing at the time. It's a little after three in the morning. I know I shouldn't call her this late, but I need this.

I hit the call button and bring the phone to my ear, listening to it ring. After a few moments, Anna's sleepy voice comes across the speaker.

"Rex? Is everything okay?" she asks, concern lacing her tone.

"Yeah, everything's fine. I'm sorry for calling so late, I just... I needed to talk to you."

There's a brief pause, and I can hear the rustle of sheets as she sits up in bed. "It's okay. What's going on?"

I rub a hand over my face, suddenly feeling foolish for waking her up in the middle of the night.

"I'm sorry, I shouldn't have called. I know you need your sleep."

"Rex, it's fine. I told you to call whenever you could. I'm glad you did."

I let out a heavy sigh, sinking back into the pillows.

"I just... I've been thinking about what you told me. About that bastard being the one who hurt you the most."

Anna is quiet for a moment, and I can almost see her biting her lip, the way she does when she's trying to find the right words.

"I'm sorry, I shouldn't have told you that. Not when you're in the middle of all this."

"No, don't apologize. But I need to hear it, Anna. I need to know what he did to you, so I can make sure he pays for it."

"Rex..." she starts, but I cut her off.

"Anna, that son of a bitch is going to pay for what he did to you. I'll make damn sure he experiences every ounce of pain and suffering he inflicted on you. I want him to know, deep in his fuckin' bones, exactly why it is happening to him. I need him to feel the weight of his sins before I finally put a bullet between his eyes and bury the bastard six feet under. He's going to regret the day he ever laid a finger on you. That's a fucking promise."

I feel terrible for putting this on her shoulders. But I need to hear it from her own lips, need that fuel to ignite the rage burning inside me.

"I'm sorry, Anna. I know this isn't fair to you," I murmur, my voice thick with restraint. "But I need you to tell me something. Just one thing that sick fuck did to you in that basement. I need to hear it."

The line goes silent save for Anna's shaky breaths. For a moment, I think she's going to refuse, that I've crossed a line by asking this of her. But then her voice comes through, small yet resolute.

"The last night... before you found me," she begins. "He came down to the basement drunk. Angrier than I'd ever seen him before..."

The rawness in Anna's voice catches in her throat as she continues, her words barely a whisper. "He beat me so badly that night, Rex. He beat me like I was nothing. Like I was less than human. He told me that I deserved it for being such a whore. Each hit left more than just a bruise, they left shame and humiliation. The worst scars aren't the ones you see on the outside; they are the ones I feel on the inside."

I squeezed my phone tightly against my ear, trying to absorb every word of Anna's trembling voice. She told me in graphic detail about the horrors she had suffered at the hands of that vile prick. My fists clenched and my heart raced with anger as I struggled to keep my emotions in check.

Recollections of seeing her for the first time came back to me. Her entire body was covered in bruises. Some already fading to a yellowish hue. Others were fresh, raw shades of purple and red. I now know those were where Ruso's fists had landed across her perfect body. Her beautiful face was swollen and her lip split, dried blood caked the corners of her mouth. But it was her eyes. Those beautiful dark eyes were shadowed with pain and fear.

"He broke my ribs that night. He..." Anna's whispered confessions trailed off. She didn't have to finish. I know what that mother fucker did to her. Violated her, took from her what no man has a right to take from a woman.

"He left me lying there, bleeding and broken. That was the moment I finally gave up. If you and the club hadn't showed up the next day, I would be dead. You carrying me out of there was the only thing that saved me. I wasn't strong enough to carry myself anymore, but you gave me your strength. You pulled me through when I didn't have the will to fight anymore, you saved me."

My throat tightened as I listened to her words. I would do whatever it took to make him pay for what he had done to her.

"He will suffer, Anna," I murmured, my voice thick with emotion. "I promise you that he will pay in blood for what he's done to you. No one hurts you and gets away with it ever again, you hear me? Never again."

Anna let out a shaky sigh as she spoke. "I just... I need you to stay safe, Rex. You coming home safe and whole is more important to me than getting revenge. Please promise me you'll be careful."

Her concern touched me, but I wouldn't let it hold me back from seeking vengeance for her. "Don't worry about me, I'll be fine. I will make him pay for his sins against you, and then I'll come back to you. I can give you both baby, that's my promise to you."

There was a moment of silence on the other end of the line, and then Anna's voice came through again, her tone soft and gentle.

"Thank you, Rex. Thank you for everything you've done for me and went through with me."

"You're welcome, sweetheart. Thank you for telling me. I'll be home soon." With that, I ended the call and lay back down on the bed, my mind racing with thoughts of vengeance and retribution.

And as I slept, I dreamed of the day when I would finally be able to look into Anna's eyes and tell her that I had kept my promise to her. That I had made that son of a bitch pay.

The conversation with Anna tonight was exactly what I needed. It reminded me why I'm here, of my purpose, and the justification for the violence yet to come.

The moment Ruso put his hands on Anna, he signed his own death warrant, and I am the executioner.

CHAPTER 14

Rex

The early evening sun casts long shadows across the motel room as I perform my final weapons check. My fingers glide over the cool metal of my 1911, checking that the magazine is fully loaded and there's one in the chamber. The silencer is threaded tightly on the barrel of the gun.

Beside it rests my blade of choice, a Ka-Bar knife. Its blade sharpened to a razor's edge. These tools of violence have become extensions of myself over the years. From my time in the Army to joining the Rebel Sons, they are brutal but sometimes necessary tools in the world I live in.

I glance over at Dom who is meticulously going over his own gear. It's impressive to see how far the kid has come. When he first started prospecting for the club, he was all bravado and enthusiasm. He's still got that fire, but it's been tempered by experience. He knows now this life ain't all fun and games.

X steps out of the bathroom, towel drying his hair. Despite his imposing stature, there's a fluid grace to his movements, the hallmark of a skilled operator. We've been through enough shit together for me to know I can trust him to have my back without question.

"You good, brother?" I ask, my voice a low rumble.

X meets my gaze and gives a curt nod. "Let's get this done."

The three of us gather around the table, spreading out the blueprints Jax provided. I trace my finger along the layout, committing every exit, hallway, and choke point to memory.

"Alright, we know Ruso's routine like the back of our hands at this point. He strolls into the club around 11:30 PM every night with his usual bodyguard."

I continue briefing them on the plan, clearly outlining each person's role and responsibilities with precision. There's no room for error or hesitation tonight. We're the spearhead driving into the heart of the Moretti organization's west coast operations. Failure is not an option for us.

As the sky outside gradually darkens, an eerie calm settles over the motel room. This is the moment we've been waiting for. The first strike in an escalating war against those who've wronged our family. I can feel the coiled tension in my muscles, the heated thrum of my pulse echoing in my ears.

One by one, we begin strapping on our gear - body armor, comms, sidearms. The weight of it all is grounding, familiar. This is who we are. What we were born for.

Finally, I turn to Dom and X, their expressions serious and resolute. "You boys ready to get to work?"

"Oh, I was born ready." A feral grin spreads across Dom's face as he checks his weapons one more time.

X simply gives a single, solemn nod.

Exhaling a deep breath, I shoulder my bag and head for the door. It's go time.

* * *

The sleek black SUV pulls up to the curb outside the Black Lotus, its engine purring like a predatory cat. I watch through narrowed eyes as Ruso steps out, escorted by his ever-present bodyguard. The man moves with the arrogant swagger of someone who believes he's untouchable. We'll see about that.

I turn to Dom, my voice low and intense. "Remember, kid. You watch Ruso. He'll motion for Velvet, and they'll head to the private room. When that happens, you send a text that it's go time."

Dom nods, his jaw set with determination.

"Start a fight at the front of the bar," I continue. "Make sure you get everyone's attention. Then, when you get tossed, you're on lookout."

A ghost of a smirk flickers across my face. "And DO NOT..."

"Do not fucking shoot you, yeah, I got it boss."

With a curt nod, I send Dom around to the front of the building. I watch him go, a mixture of pride and apprehension swirling in my gut. The kid's grown up, but this is the big leagues. No room for rookie mistakes.

I check my watch, the seconds ticking down like a countdown to detonation. X already in position, ready to cut the security feed on my signal.

The anticipation is a living thing, coiled in my muscles, thrumming through my veins. Every sense is heightened, every nerve ending alive and screaming for action.

My phone vibrates in my pocket about 45 minutes later. Dom's signal. It's go time. I whistle at X, so he knows to cut the feed.

I slip around to the back of the building, my footsteps silent on the pavement. The music pulses through the walls, masking any sound of my approach.

I pause at the back door, my hand resting on the handle. One deep breath in, then out. X is beside me seconds later. Showtime.

I push open the back door, X right on my heels. The pounding base of the club music envelops us as we slip inside. My eyes rapidly adjust to the low lighting, scanning for threats.

We move in a silent, deadly tandem born from years of operating together. Down the hallway, through the employee area, clearing each corner with precise sweeps of our weapons.

Up ahead, a lone guard stands watch outside Ruso's private room, just like clockwork. X gives me a subtle nod and we accelerate into position on either side of the hallway.

In one fluid motion, I lash out with my left arm, clamping the guard in a vise-grip choke while X relieves him of his sidearm. The man's eyes bulge in shock as I effortlessly cut off his airway.

With his struggles weakening, we hustle him into a nearby supply closet. X pins him against the wall as I press the silenced muzzle of my 1911 against the guard's forehead. Our eyes lock for the briefest moment. He knows what's coming. There's no fear, just acceptance.

I squeeze the trigger without hesitation. The suppressed gunshot is barely audible over the music's thunderous cadence. The guard crumples to the floor in a lifeless heap.

Stepping back into the hallway, I meet X's unflinching stare and gesture for him to move by the door of the room Ruso is currently inside of. He takes the dead bodyguard's place, standing sentry outside the door.

My heart pounds in my ears, not from fear or adrenaline, but pure, distilled fury. This is for Anna. For every ounce of pain and degradation inflicted on her by that sadistic piece of shit. With a steadying exhale, I grip the door handle and quietly push it open.

I step into the dimly lit room, the heavy scent of cigars and whiskey hanging thick in the air. Ruso is there, seated on a plush leather couch, the top few buttons of his silk shirt undone. His face registers shock for the briefest moment before that familiar smug mask slides back into place. Velvet scurries from the room picking up her clothes as quickly as she can as she goes.

"Well, well..." He drawls, eyeing me with a mixture of contempt and curiosity. "If it isn't the big, bad Rebel dog himself."

I remain silent, letting the muzzle of my pistol do the talking as I level it squarely at his head. Ruso seems to get the message loud and clear.

"Hey now, let's not do anything rash here." That oily smile spreads across his face as he raises his hands in mock surrender.

"Whatever you are getting paid for this, I can double it. Triple it, even."

His eyes flit around the room, desperately seeking any avenue of escape or negotiation. When he finds none, the bravado falters slightly.

"You don't want to do this. I'm a made man. My family, they'll come for you and anyone you care about. Even that sweet little daughter of yours won't be..."

The words freeze in his throat as I take a single step forward, the pistol unwavering. A bead of sweat trickles down the side of Ruso's face.

"You so much as say her name..." I growl, each word carrying the weight of a death sentence.

"And the only thing your family's gonna get is what's left of you in a goddamn Ziplock."

Ruso's mouth works soundlessly for a moment before snapping shut. The fear is naked in his eyes now, stripped of all bravado. He knows I'm not bluffing. Not this time.

I can almost taste the metallic tang of his terror. It's intoxicating, addictive, the ultimate high for a predator like me. To have such power, such control over someone's life. To decide, with the single twitch of my trigger finger, whether they get to take another breath or not.

Part of me wants to draw this out, to make the bastard beg and grovel for every anguished second. To make him feel even a fraction of the suffering Anna endured. But I can't give in to that hunger, that gnawing bloodlust. Not tonight. This has to be clinical, efficient.

I take another step forward, the pistol's barrel now mere inches from Ruso's sweaty forehead. His eyes are wild, animalistic.

"This is for Anna," I say, my voice little more than a guttural rasp. "And every other poor soul you and your kind have tormented."

Ruso opens his mouth, perhaps to beg or bargain once more. But any words he might have uttered are cut short when I press my pistol against Ruso's forehead, finger curled around the trigger. But I hesitate. It's too easy, too quick. This scum doesn't deserve a clean death, not after what he did to Anna.

I lower the gun and holster it, a grim smile spreading across my face. Ruso's eyes widen in confusion, then fear as I lunge forward, driving my fist into his gut. He doubles over, gasping for breath.

"You're gonna pay for every scar, every bruise you left on her," I growl, punctuating each word with another vicious blow.

Ruso staggers back, his face a mask of pain and rage. He swings wildly, trying to connect, but I dodge easily. I've been waiting for this moment, dreaming of it.

We trade blows in a brutal dance, fists and elbows colliding with flesh and bone. Ruso's good, I'll give him that. But he's fighting for his life. I'm fighting for something more.

I hear Ann's voice on repeat in my head, "the worst scars aren't the ones you see on the outside; they are the ones I feel on the inside." The fury I feel is a living, breathing beast inside me now. It's on a rampage, taking over my every move, driving each punishing blow.

Ruso's attacks grow desperate, sloppy. He's tired, his breaths coming in ragged gasps. I seize my chance, sweeping his legs out from under him. He crashes to the floor, dazed. I'm on him in an instant, straddling his chest. My hands wrap around his throat, squeezing, feeling his pulse flutter beneath my fingers.

It's still not enough. I need him to suffer, to feel the same helpless terror Anna must have felt. Releasing his throat, I shift my grip to his face. My thumbs hover over his eyes, trembling with barely restrained rage.

"This is for her," I snarl. And then I plunge my thumbs into his eye sockets.

Ruso screams an unhuman howl of agony. I feel the wet pop as his eyeballs rupture, feel the warm gush of blood and viscous fluid over my hands. And still, I press deeper, grinding, pulverizing, until his screams fade to pathetic moans of suffering.

I rise to my feet, my breath coming in ragged gasps, hands slick with Ruso's blood. The sight of him lying there, face a ruined mess, fills me with a grim satisfaction. But it's still not enough. It'll never be enough to make up for what he did to Anna.

I walk over to the door and grab the small bag of goodies Jake had packed me for this very occasion. Digging through, I spot a hammer and a pair of small gardening sheers. I return to Ruso lying on the floor and I grab one of his hands. His fear is heightened by the fact he can't see what's about to happen. It fills me with a sick pleasure to see the terrified look on what's left his face.

“You like nursery rhymes Vinnie? I fuckin' love them, let me tell you my favorite.” Holding his thumb out from the rest of his fingers on his left hand, I began.

“This little piggie went to market.” With a sadistic grin, I recited the nursery rhyme. The rusty metal of the gardening sheers glinted in the dim light as I cut through flesh and bone, each snap and crunch sending shivers of delight down my spine. Ruso's screams only fueled my bloodlust, spurring me on to sever his thumb and let it fall to the floor with a sickening, wet thud. His futile attempts to escape and cries for mercy were like music to my ears, a symphony of pain and terror. This little piggie went to market indeed.

I continued reciting the nursery rhyme, “this little piggy stayed home,” as I spread his hand out beside him. Focusing on just the index finger, and I began pounding with the hammer. With each strike bones shattered and flesh tore, leaving nothing but a mangled mess of tissue and crushed bone.

As beautiful as it was to hear, Ruso’s incessant crying was really starting to piss me off. “What’s wrong Vinny, you don’t like my games? I really thought I was putting a nice twist on this for you.” A grin spread across my face, “wait till you see how I play ‘Ring Around the Rosie’.”

I glance at my watch and see the seconds ticking down. Dom and X can only keep the security occupied for so long.

"Too bad Vinny, it seems our time together is up."

I draw my sidearm once more, the weight of it familiar and reassuring in my blood-slicked hand. As much as I want to drag this out, to make Ruso suffer for an eternity, I know my time is limited. The clock's ticking, and we need to be gone before the cops show.

Ruso writhes on the floor, his good hand clawing at his ruined face, choked sobs escaping his throat. I stand over him, pistol aimed at his head, finger curled around the trigger.

"This is for Anna," I growl, my voice barely recognizable to my own ears. "And for every other woman whose life you destroyed."

Ruso's head lolls in my direction, his breathing ragged and wet. "Please..." he croaks, the word garbled by the blood filling his mouth. "Please don't..."

With my finger wrapped tightly around the trigger, I squeeze, and the gun releases a muffled bang. In an instant, it's done. Ruso's body goes limp, and a dark puddle of blood pools beneath his head.

For a moment, I stand there, my breath labored and my hands trembling, staring down at the lifeless body of the monster I've slain. A feeling of gratification washing over me. As I look down at my hand holding my gun, still dripping with blood, I know justice has been served. I promised Anna he would pay and pay he did. One promise down, one to go.

CHAPTER 15

Rex

We pull out of the back parking lot behind the Black Lotus, following formation. I'm in the front, X behind me, Dom bringing up the rear. My bike's engine rumbles beneath me, the familiar vibration grounding me after the intensity of the past hour.

We hit the streets, weaving through the late-night traffic. My mind is still buzzing, replaying the confrontation with Ruso over and over. The wet crunch of his eyeballs rupturing. His sobbing as I pulverized his finger with the hammer. I feel nothing but satisfaction.

About four blocks from the strip club, red and blue lights flare in my rearview mirror. *Fuck.*

I pull over to the side of the road, my heart pounding in my chest. X and Dom drive past and I see them pull over and park about a block down the street. There's no way the cops could know what I did yet unless there were security cameras we didn't know about tied to another feed.

The flashing lights reflect off my side mirrors as it pulls up behind me. I kill the engine and rest my hands on the handlebars, taking a deep breath to compose myself. In the mirror, I watch as the officer exits his vehicle and starts approaching.

"Evening," he calls out as he nears my bike. "Is this a custom bike?"

"Yes sir, I built her myself," I reply, proud despite the tightness in my chest.

"Damn fine work." The officer nods, then his expression turns more serious. "You know why I pulled you over?"

"No sir, I don't," I reply, keeping my voice steady. "I wasn't speeding, and my tags are up to date."

The officer nods, then gestures down the street in the direction I came from. "I saw you make a right turn onto this street. Your front turn signal is working, but your back signal isn't."

Shit. I hadn't even noticed. With everything else on my mind, a busted turn signal was the last thing I was thinking about.

"Can I see your license and registration, please?" the officer asks, his tone professional but firm. I nod, trying to keep my movements slow and deliberate.

"Sure thing, officer. They're in my saddlebag here." As I reach for the saddlebag on the opposite side of my bike from where the cop is standing, I send up a silent prayer of thanks. My 1911 and Ka-Bar knife are stuffed down inside, hidden from his view.

I pull out my wallet and registration, handing them over to the officer. I'm acutely aware of Ruso's blood drying on my hands beneath my gloves. He takes them, examining them closely under the streetlight.

"Rex Riggs," he reads aloud, then glances up at me. "You're a long way from Montana, Mr. Riggs. What brings you to Portland?"

I force a casual shrug, my mind racing for a plausible excuse. "Just visiting some old friends," I lie smoothly. "Thought I'd take a little road trip, see some new sights."

The officer nods slowly, his eyes still fixed on my papers. Every second feels like an eternity as I wait for him to hand them back.

The cop's radio crackles to life, the dispatcher's voice cutting through the tense silence. "All available units, please respond. Reports of two D.O.A.'s at the Black Lotus gentlemen's club. Repeat, two confirmed D.O.A's. All available units please respond."

My heart nearly stops in my chest. They found the bodies already. I keep my expression neutral, but my mind is reeling. I need to get the hell out of here before they connect me to the scene.

The officer's eyes narrow as he listens to the dispatch. He glances back at me, suspicion written all over his face.

"You said you were just passing through, right? Visiting friends? You didn't stop by the Black Lotus tonight?"

I nod, my mouth suddenly dry. "That's right, officer. Just got into town a couple hours ago."

The officer's eyes bore into mine, his suspicion growing by the second. "Mr. Riggs, I'm going to ask you again. Have you been to the Black Lotus tonight?"

My heart pounds in my chest, but I keep my expression neutral. "No, sir. Like I said, I just got into town. Haven't had a chance to hit up any clubs yet."

He nods slowly, but I can tell he doesn't believe me. "Funny thing is, dispatch just reported two dead bodies found at that very club. And here you are, just a few blocks away."

I swallow hard, my mind racing for an explanation. "That's a hell of a coincidence, officer. But I had nothing to do with it."

"Mind if I take a look in your saddlebags then?" he asks, his tone making it clear it's not a request.

I hesitate for a split second, knowing my weapons are hidden inside. If he finds them, I'm fucked. But if I refuse, it'll only make me look more guilty.

"Go ahead," I say, trying to keep my voice steady. "I've got nothing to hide."

The officer steps closer to my bike, his hand resting on the butt of his gun. He reaches for the saddlebag, and I hold my breath, praying he doesn't find the 1911 or the Ka-Bar.

But luck isn't on my side tonight. He unzips the bag and peers inside, his eyes widening as he spots the weapons. "Well, well, what do we have here?" he says, pulling out the gun and holding it up to the light.

"I have a permit for that," I say quickly, but it's a weak excuse and we both know it.

"I'm sure you do," he replies, his tone dripping with sarcasm. "But that doesn't explain why you're carrying it around the same night two people turn up dead at a nearby strip club."

He reaches for his radio, his eyes never leaving mine. "Dispatch, this is Officer Jameson. I've got a suspect in custody in connection with the Black Lotus homicides. Requesting backup at my location."

My heart sinks as I realize what's happening. I'm being arrested for murder, and there's not a damn thing I can do about it.

The officer pulls out his handcuffs, gesturing for me to get off my bike. "Rex Riggs, you're under arrest for the murders of Vincent Ruso and Marco Ferrara. You have the right to remain silent. Anything you say, can and will be used against you in a court of law..."

The officer's words hit me like a sucker punch to the gut. How the hell did he know Ruso's name? That hadn't been mentioned on the radio. Something wasn't adding up here. I narrow my eyes at him, my suspicion growing by the second.

"Hold up. You said the names of the victims. But that wasn't said over the radio. How do you know their names if dispatch never mentioned them?"

Officer Jameson falters for a split second, a flicker of uncertainty crossing his face. But he quickly regains his composure, shaking his head dismissively.

"It doesn't matter. Point is, you're under arrest for their murders."

This whole situation feels off, like I'm being set up. And now this cop slips up and reveals he knows more than he should?

"Bullshit," I growl, taking a step towards him. "You're hiding something. What do you know? And how the fuck did you know their names?"

Jameson's hand tightens on his gun, his eyes hardening. "I'm asking the questions here, Riggs. Not you. Now turn around and put your hands behind your back."

I'm not going down without a fight. "Not until you tell me what's really going on here. Who are you working for? Moretti? Someone else?"

The officer's jaw clenches, a vein throbbing in his temple. "I said, turn around and put your hands behind your back. Don't make me force you."

I stand my ground, my fists clenched at my sides. "You're gonna have to, because I'm not going anywhere until I get some fucking answers."

Jameson takes a menacing step forward, his hand moving to the taser on his belt. "Last chance, Riggs. Comply or I'll make you comply."

I can see in his eyes that he's not bluffing. But I'll be damned if I'm going down without knowing the truth. I brace myself for a fight, ready to do whatever it takes.

"Give it your best shot, you piece of shit," I snarl, raising my fists. "Let's see what you got." And with that, all hell breaks loose.

I stand my ground, fists raised as the corrupt cop advances on me. Every muscle in my body is tensed, ready for the fight I know is coming.

"Last chance, Riggs," Jameson snarls, his hand hovering over the taser on his belt. "Make this easy on yourself."

I bare my teeth in a feral grin. "Not a chance, you lying bastard. I want answers first."

That's all it takes for him to snap. In one fluid motion, Jameson draws his taser and fires. But I'm ready for him. I twist out of the way at the last second, the barbs whizzing past my face.

"Nice try!" I taunt as I lunge forward, driving my fist into his gut.

Jameson doubles over with a pained grunt, but he recovers

quickly. He swings his taser at me, but I bat it aside and deliver a bone-crunching elbow to his face. Blood spurts from his shattered nose as he staggers back.

"Who are you working for?" I demand, pressing my advantage. "Talk!"

Instead of answering, Jameson reaches for his gun. Big mistake. I close the distance between us and slam my fist into his wrist, knocking the weapon free. It clatters to the ground as I grab him by the collar and hurl him against the nearest wall.

"I'm not asking again," I snarl, pinning him there with my forearm across his throat. "Who sent you? Moretti?"

Jameson coughs and wheezes, his eyes bulging. For a second, I think he's not going to break. Then he gives the slightest nod.

"Fuck," I mutter, my grip loosening slightly. I should've known Tony would have eyes everywhere. He must've known I was planning on taking out Ruso and let it happen to set me up.

Jameson seizes the opportunity, driving his knee up into my groin. White-hot pain lances through me and I stagger back, gasping for breath.

The corrupt cop dives for his fallen gun, but I manage to kick it away before he can grab it. He whirls on me, fists raised, a crazed look in his eyes.

"You're going down for this, Riggs," he spits, circling me like a hungry shark. "The Moretti's are going to gut you and your whole club."

I grin through the pain, wiping blood from my split lip. "Is that so? You can tell Tony that he's next on my list."

I look up to see X and Dom racing over on their bikes.

"Jesus, Rex," Dom says, his eyes wide as he takes in the scene. "What the fuck?"

I spit out a mouthful of blood, glaring at Jameson's smug face as he stands there gloating. Just as I'm about to lunge at him again, the wail of sirens cuts through the air.

"Backup's here," Jameson sneers, straightening his uniform. "You're fucked now, Riggs."

I glance over my shoulder to see X and Dom dismounting their bikes, concern etched on their faces as they take in the scene.

"Rex, what the hell happened?" X demands, striding over.

Before I can answer, three squad cars come screeching to a halt, blocking us in. Officers pour out, weapons drawn and trained on us.

"On the ground, now!" one of them barks. "Hands where I can see them!"

I hesitate for a split second, weighing my options. But with a dozen guns pointed at us, I know we don't have a choice. Slowly,

I raise my hands and sink to my knees.

X and Dom follow suit, exchanging looks as the cops swarm in. Rough hands yank my arms behind my back, the cold metal biting into my wrists as they cuff me.

"Rex Riggs, you're under arrest," Jameson says triumphantly, looming over me. "For the murders of Vincent Ruso and Marco Ferrara, and for assaulting an officer."

"Fuck you," I snarl, struggling against the cuffs. "You set me up, you lying piece of shit!"

But it's no use. The other officers haul me to my feet, dragging me towards a waiting squad car. I catch a glimpse of X and Dom being similarly manhandled, their faces tight with anger and frustration.

As they shove me into the backseat, I meet Jameson's gaze one last time. There's a smug satisfaction in his eyes that pisses me the fuck off.

"This isn't over," I growl, holding his stare. "Not by a long shot."

He just smirks as he slams the door in my face. The car lurches into motion, carrying me further away from my bike, my brothers, and my freedom.

As the reality of the situation sinks in, my mind is racing. Jameson's slip-up about knowing the victims' names is the key. If I can prove he's working for Moretti, maybe I can get these charges dropped.

It's a long shot, but it's my only play. As the sound of sirens fades away, I lean my head back against the seat and shut my eyes and begin strategizing my next move. I will make sure that corrupt bastard pays, along with Moretti for trying to set me up. They have no idea who they're fucking with, but they're about to find out the hard way.

I think about Anna and Emmalynn waiting for me back home. I promised them I'd be back soon, but now it looks like I might not be able to keep that promise. The thought of leaving them alone, kills me. I send up a silent prayer, hoping this isn't the end of the road for me. That somehow, someway, there is a way for me to find my way back to the family I love.

CHAPTER 16

Anna

I'm coloring with Emmalynn at my little desk in the office, trying my best to stay inside the lines of the picture she's given me. The tip of my tongue pokes out in concentration as I carefully fill in each section. Emmalynn giggles beside me, her small hands moving rapidly with a rainbow of crayons.

"You're doing great, Anna!" she encourages me, always so sweet.

I smile at her, feeling a warmth bloom in my chest. These quiet moments with her are precious, a stark contrast to the darkness I've known. My phone rings, an unknown number flashing on the screen. I quickly answer, not wanting to miss any updates while Rex is away.

"This is a collect call from an inmate, Rex, at the Multnomah County Jail. Will you accept the charges?"

The words hit me like a physical blow, stealing my breath. Rex… is in jail? Panic claws at my throat as my mind races. What could have happened? Is he okay? Without hesitation, I accept the charges, desperate to hear his voice. I grab Emmalynn's hand, crayons clattering to the floor as I jerk upright.

"Come on, sweetie, we need to go find uncle Jax." Her eyes widen at the urgency in my voice, but she doesn't question it, simply allowing me to lead her out of the office. My heart thunders in my ears as we hurry across the compound toward the clubhouse.

Rex's voice crackles through the phone. "Hey, it's me. How are you two doing?"

Relief washes over me at the sound of him, solid and reassuring despite the circumstances.

"We're okay. Em's been an angel as always." I swallow hard, forcing myself to remain calm for her sake. "Rex, what's happening? Why are you calling from... there?"

He exhales heavily. "Em can hear you right now?"

"Yeah, we are walking over to the clubhouse to find Jax. I figured he might need to know some of the things you're about to tell me."

“Yeah, baby he does. Things got... complicated after. I can't go into details right now, but I'm not going to make it home today. I'm so sorry."

My steps falter at his words, dread settling like a stone in my stomach. Emmalynn tugs on my hand, peering up at me with those big, innocent eyes that haven't witnessed the true cruelty of this world yet. Not like I have.

"It's okay, I understand," I murmur into the phone. "Just be careful and take care of yourself, okay? We'll be here waiting."

“Anna, I need to ask you a favor. I need you to have Jax get ahold of my dad soon before he leaves the Portland area. He needs to get a lawyer for X, Dom, and me.”

I grip the phone tighter, Rex's words echoing in my ear as I make my way to the clubhouse with Emmalynn in tow. My heart races, fear and worry threatening to overwhelm me, but I force myself to focus on what needs to be done.

"Of course, I'll get in touch with Beau right away."

Rex's relief is palpable, even through the crackling prison phone line.

"Thank you, Anna." He pauses, and I can almost see him running a hand over his face, the weight of the world on his shoulders. "Make sure you tell him to come see me as soon as he can. There's a lot he needs to know, stuff that the lawyer will need to be aware of."

"I'll make sure he gets the message," I promise, my mind already racing with the tasks ahead. "I'll have Jax start looking into the best criminal defense attorney in the Portland area. We'll get you guys out of there, Rex."

Emmalynn tugs on my hand, her little face scrunched up in confusion.

"Is daddy okay?" she asks, her voice small and unsure.

I nod solemnly at Emmalynn, pulling her close to me.

"Your daddy's fine, sweetheart, but he's in a bit of a situation right now with work. Do you want to talk to him?"

Her eyes widen and she nods vigorously. I switch the phone to speaker mode and hand it to her.

"Daddy?"

"Hey there, princess. Are you being a good girl for Anna?" Rex's voice is thick with emotion.

"Yes, daddy," Emmalynn replies dutifully. "When are you coming home? I miss you."

There's a pause on the other end, and I can practically see Rex's internal struggle as he tries to find the right words. He clears his throat before he speaks.

"I'm not sure, baby girl. I messed up and made a big mess of my job, so I have to stay here for a little while to try to fix it."

Emmalynn's little face scrunches in confusion. "Like time-out? Did you do something bad?"

Rex lets out a soft chuckle, but it's tinged with sadness.

"Yeah, kind of like a time-out for grown-ups. But I'm going to be okay, I promise. Anna and the guys are going to help me get out of time out as soon as they can."

"Okay, daddy, love you." Emmalynn says, her voice small but trusting. She hands the phone back to me, her lower lip trembling ever so slightly.

I scoop her up in my arms, cradling her against me as I bring the phone back to my ear.

"Rex? You still there?"

"Yeah, I'm here," he rasps, and I can hear the strain in his voice. "Anna, I... thank you. For everything. I don't know what I'd do without you right now."

My throat tightens with emotion, and I have to blink back tears.

"You don't have to thank me, Rex. We're family, remember? We take care of each other, no matter what."

There's a pause, and then he speaks again, his voice low and intense.

"I need you to promise me something. If things go sideways... I need you to take care of Em. Make sure she stays safe and none of this ever touches her. Can you do that for me? I know it's a lot to ask."

A chill runs down my spine at the gravity of his words.

"Rex, of course. You're the only reason I'm still standing. I'll do anything you need me to do."

"Anna," desperation creeping into his tone. "She's all I have left. I can't lose her too."

I swallow hard, my arms tightening around Emmalynn's small frame.

"Okay," I whisper, my voice trembling. "I promise. But Rex, she's not all you have left. You'll be home before you know it, and we both will be here waiting."

There's a commotion on his end, and Rex lets out a weary sigh.

"I've gotta go. Take care of my girl, Anna. Miss you both."

The line goes dead, leaving me standing there with Emmalynn in my arms, her head resting trustingly against my shoulder. A fierce protectiveness surges through me, mingling with fear and determination.

Whatever happens, I won't let Rex down. I'll keep his little girl safe, no matter what it takes. I never had anyone looking out for me when I was Emmalynn's age and I'll be damned if I'd ever let anything happen to this little girl. With renewed purpose, I stride toward the clubhouse, in search of Jax.

Pops and Ox are in the common room of the clubhouse playing pool.

"Do you guys know where Jax is? It's important that I talk to him right now. It's for Rex."

"I haven't seen him today, honey. He's probably holed up in the basement with all his screens and keyboards. Everything okay?" Ox eyes me and then Emmalynn, nothing but concern on his face.

"No Ox, it's not." I nod my head towards Emmalynn, "but I can't talk right now. Can you two keep an eye on Em for me while I find Jax? I'll have him fill you in afterwards."

"No problem." Pops walks over and picks up Em. "You wanna have a beer with Pops?"

"Pop Pop, you're so silly." Em giggles.

"Thank you," I toss over my shoulder as I make my way to Jax's command center in the basement, knocking on the door.

"Jax??? Are you in there?"

"Yeah babe, come in."

I practically sprint across the room to where he is sitting in front of a row of monitors and keyboards.

"Can you help me get ahold of Beau please? I don't have his number. I need to talk to him now." I'm starting to get a little frantic now that I don't have to keep calm in front of Emmalynn.

"Slow down, Anna. What's wrong? He's got a bit of a situation right now at the docks. I can help you."

I begin shaking my head before he even finishes speaking.

"Rex, X, and Dom have all been arrested in Portland. Rex said he needs Beau to go see him before he leaves Portland. He has information that a lawyer needs to know. I need you to find the best criminal defense attorney you can find and hire them for all three of them. The money the club got from hitting Regali alone should more than cover any legal fees and bail if they get it."

"Fuck, okay. Let's call him."

I sit on a worn leather chair in Jax's command center, my leg bouncing nervously as he types furiously on his keyboard. The dim lighting and the hum of the computers only add to the sense of urgency that hangs in the air.

"I'm pulling up a list of the top criminal defense attorneys in Portland now," Jax says, his eyes glued to the screen. "I'll start making calls, see who's available to take on a case like this."

I nod, my throat too tight to speak. The reality of the situation is starting to sink in, and I can feel the panic rising in my chest. Rex, X, and Dom are all behind bars, facing God knows what charges. And here I am, helpless to do anything but wait. Jax must sense my distress, because he reaches over and squeezes my hand.

"We'll get them out of there, Anna. I promise. The club takes care of its own."

I manage a weak smile, grateful for his reassurance. But the knot in my stomach doesn't ease. I can't shake the feeling that this is just the beginning, that the worst is yet to come.

As if on cue, Jax's phone rings. He snatches it up, his face grim.

"Yeah, Beau. I heard." A pause, then, "Anna's here with me now. We're working on getting them representation."

I lean forward, straining to hear Beau's response. But Jax just nods, his expression unreadable.

"Okay, I'll let her know. Keep us updated." He hangs up, turning to face me with a sigh. "Beau is on his way into Portland now. He'll see Rex as soon as he can and find out what's going on."

Relief washes over me, followed quickly by a fresh wave of anxiety.

"What do you think Rex needs to tell him? What could be so important that it can't wait?"

Jax shakes his head, his brow furrowed.

"I don't know, but it can't be good. If Rex is worried about the lawyer needing to know something..." He trails off, the implication clear.

I swallow hard, my mind racing with possibilities. What if they found evidence linking Rex to Ruso's murder? What if someone saw him that night? The thought makes my blood run cold.

"We have to get them out of there, Jax," I whisper, my voice shaking. "Whatever it takes. We can't let them go down for this. They were all there because of me. If Em has to grow up without her dad..." I pause to regain my composure trying not to cry. "It's all on me."

I can't stop pacing the length of the room, my mind spinning with worst-case scenarios. The weight of guilt presses down on my chest, making it hard to breathe. Rex, X, and Dom, they're all in this mess because of me. Because they were trying to protect me, to avenge what was done to me.

Jax is still on the phone, his voice low and urgent as he talks to one criminal defense attorney after another. I catch snippets of the conversations, aggravated assault, possible homicide charges, bail hearing, each word hitting me like a physical blow.

I think of Emmalynn upstairs with Pops and Ox, blissfully unaware of the danger her father is in. The thought of her growing up without him, of Rex spending years behind bars because of me... it's too much to bear.

"I need some air," I mutter to Jax, not waiting for a response before I'm bolting up the stairs and out of the clubhouse.

The cool evening breeze hits my face as I step outside, but it does nothing to calm the storm raging inside me. I lean against the wall, closing my eyes and trying to steady my breathing. I don't know how long I stand there, lost in my own desperate prayers. But eventually, I feel a hand on my shoulder, startling me out of my thoughts.

It's Jax, his face lined with worry as he hands me his cell phone.

"Anna, Beau's on the phone. He just got back from seeing Rex."

My heart leaps into my throat. I put the phone to my ear.

"Beau? How is he? What did he say?" I hear Beau sigh into the phone.

"It's not good, sweetheart. They're looking at some serious charges. But Rex, he's... he's more worried about you and Emmalynn than anything else."

Tears sting my eyes, and I blink them back furiously.

"This is all my fault, Beau. They're in there because of me."

His voice turns stern. "No, Anna. This is on Moretti, on the evil bastards who hurt you. Not you, never you."

But even as he says the words, I can't quite bring myself to believe them. The guilt is too heavy, the fear too real. All I can do is hope that somehow, someway, we'll find a way to bring our boys home.

CHAPTER 17

Rex

The metal door of the private interview room in the jail swings open with a heavy clang. I see my father stride in alongside a stunning redhead who I assume must be our lawyer.

She's a bombshell, no doubt. All dangerous curves and fiery hair that cascades past her shoulders. I'd guess her to be close to my age, mid 30's. But even with her killer looks, she can't hold a candle to Anna. The lawyer fixes the guard with an icy glare.

"That camera better be off, and you better not have anyone listening in on this privileged conversation," she warns, her voice dripping with authority. "Or I'll be suing this department again, for a third time."

I can't help but smirk. This woman is a shark.

"Gentlemen," she announces, placing a leather briefcase on the metal table. "I'm Victoria Price, your legal counsel." Her piercing green eyes meet mine as she extends a perfectly manicured hand. "Rex, I presume?"

I grasp her hand firmly, "yes ma'am, that's me."

Releasing her grip, she gestures to the others.

"And you must be Xavier and Dominic."

"Yes ma'am," they both say in unison. Dad clears his throat, his expression unreadable.

"Ms. Price was highly recommended. The best criminal defense attorney in the state."

"From what I understand, you were pulled over for a faulty turn signal, correct?" Victoria directs her question towards me.

I nod, shifting uncomfortably in my seat.

"Yeah, that's right. I had no idea it was out."

She waves her hand dismissively.

"That's not the issue here. The problem is, they found blood on your hands and clothing. Care to explain that?"

I feel my stomach drop. I knew this was going to come up.

"Look, I got into a fight earlier that night. Some asshole was harassing a girl at a bar, and I stepped in. Things got messy, but it was just a scuffle. Nothing serious."

Victoria raises an eyebrow, clearly not buying it.

"And this fight just happened to occur on the same night that Vincent Ruso turns up dead in the very club you were seen leaving?"

I lean back in my chair, trying to keep my expression neutral.

"I don't know anything about that. I'm telling you; I was just in the wrong place at the wrong time."

She sighs, shuffling through her papers.

"Well, unfortunately for you, the cops aren't going to see it that way. They've got circumstantial evidence linking you to the scene, and they're going to try to pin this on you."

I feel a surge of anger rising in my chest.

"So, what the hell do we do now? I'm not going down for this."

Victoria meets my gaze, her expression fierce.

"First, you cut the bullshit you're trying to feed me. I can see right through your story and even the clowns they have parading as cops around here will too. Second, we fight back. We poke holes in their case, we discredit their evidence, and we make them regret ever trying to mess with the Rebel Sons."

Damn, I think I like this woman.

"Bullshit cut, where do we go from here."

Victoria leans back in her chair, scrutinizing me through narrowed eyes.

"Beau filled me in on the basics of the case against you three. I've also pulled all the police files and reports they have so far."

She pauses, letting that sink in for a moment. I can feel the weight of her next words before she even says them.

"It won't be difficult getting the charges dropped against Xavier and Dominic. But you, Rex... your situation is more complicated."

My heart pounds in my chest as I brace myself for what's coming.

"When they searched your bike, they found a firearm in the saddlebags. A 1911 handgun and a knife. Ballistics matched that weapon to the bullets recovered from Ruso's body and the dead bodyguard."

Victoria must sense the shift in my demeanor because she leans forward intently.

"That gun and knife is the key pieces of physical evidence tying you directly to the murders. It's not going to be easy to refute. We're going to need an airtight alibi and credible witnesses to even stand a chance."

I rack my brain, trying to think of anyone who could vouch for my whereabouts that night besides X and Dom. Coming up empty, I slump back defeatedly.

"I don't have an alibi. It was just the three of us."

Dad speaks up from beside me. "Then we create one. Forge receipts, manufacture a paper trail if we have to."

"Now hold on," Victoria interjects, holding up a hand. "Let's not get ahead of ourselves with anything illegal here. Not when we still have options to explore."

Her eyes bore into mine with startling intensity.

"I need you to tell me everything, Rex. No more half-truths or twisted facts. If you were involved, I can't help you unless I know exactly what went down."

I take a deep breath, steeling myself for what I'm about to reveal.

"Alright, you want the full story? Here it is."

I recount the events of that night in vivid detail, from the intelligence we'd gathered on Ruso's routines to the carefully orchestrated plan of attack. I describe how we infiltrated the club, neutralizing security until I came face-to-face with Ruso himself.

Victoria remains silent, her expression unreadable as I depict the brutal confrontation that left Ruso a bloody, lifeless heap on the floor.

"We had the security footage loop covered, and there was only one witness. A dancer named Velvet that Ruso always took into the private rooms with him. We paid her to leave the door unlocked and then get out as soon as I went in."

I pause, letting that sink in. "So as far as anyone else knows, I could've just been another client leaving with Velvet after our... session."

Victoria nods slowly. "Interesting. And what about the cop that pulled you over? You said he seemed to piece things together based on the call from the club."

"Yeah, that's what worries me," I admit. "I'm not sure how much he figured out or already knew. He said both of the victims' names from the club when he was reading me my rights. Their names were never said over his radio. I heard everything. He knew who was killed before the bodies were found."

Her eyes narrow contemplatively.

"Okay, that's our defense. I'll go after that cop and prove he's dirty. He must have planted that gun and knife when he pulled you over, intentionally targeting you. You had a physical altercation with the arresting officer while he had the fabricated evidence in his hands. At which time the blood was transferred to you."

I nod slowly, taking in Victoria's bold strategy.

"Ma'am, he didn't actually..." I was cut off before I could finish.

"Do not finish that sentence," Victoria interjects sharply. Her eyes bore into me with an intensity that makes me shrink back slightly.

"Are you innocent?" She turns her piercing gaze towards Dom first, giving a curt nod. Dom swallows hard, his voice wavering.

"Yes...?" It comes out more like a question than an answer. Victoria doesn't seem fazed, immediately shifting her focus to X and then me, that same expectant nod following her stare.

"Yes," X and I both respond, our voices firm and resolute.

Victoria's expression doesn't change, but I can sense her carefully weighing our answers. Finally, she leans back, seeming satisfied.

"Okay then, that's all I need to know to defend you." Her tone is decisive, brooking no argument. "From here on out, anything else, unless it helps your case, I don't need to know. If it's not helpful to your case, it's not helpful to me or to you."

There's a heavy silence that follows. I can feel the weight of her words sinking in. She's laying out the ground rules. From here on out, we play by her rules if we want to beat this.

I catch my father's eye, seeing the same realization reflected back at me. This isn't some small-town public defender we're dealing with. Victoria Price is a force to be reckoned with, and she's not about to let us jeopardize her defense strategy.

Despite my initial reluctance, I can't deny the growing sense of respect for her. She may be my only hope to get out of this situation and back home with my daughter. I silently nod in agreement and show my commitment to following her conditions. No more secrets. No more deceptions. Just the truth, whichever version gives us the best chance at beating these charges and keeping the club intact.

A slight smirk tugs at the corner of my mouth. This woman is ruthless, and I love it. "You think you can make that case?"

Victoria leans back, her confidence radiating.

"Trust me, handsome. I'm very good at exposing corrupt cops. Leave it to me. I'll destroy his credibility and bury him so deep he'll never be able to dig his way back out."

I'll do whatever it takes to get back to Em and Anna. Even if it means putting my fate in the hands of this ball-busting lawyer and hoping she's as good as she thinks she is.

CHAPTER 18

Anna

I woke up the next morning to my mother knocking on my bedroom door.

"Anna, dear, Beau called with an update," she said as I rubbed the sleep from my eyes.

Sitting up in bed, I motioned for her to come in.

"What did he say?"

"Beau and the guys met with the lawyer earlier, and she is working on it. The lawyer thinks she can get X and Dom out for sure, and the charges dropped, but Rex won't be as easy." My heart sank at those words.

"Why is Rex's case more difficult?" I felt a lump form in my throat as worry washed over me. Mom sat down on the edge of the bed, taking my hand in hers.

"Apparently, the police found what they believe are the murder weapons in Rex's saddlebags when he was pulled over. A gun and a knife, both with traces of the victim's blood." I shook my head in disbelief.

"I know, honey. It doesn't sound good. Beau said the lawyer is working on a defense strategy, claiming the cop who arrested Rex planted that evidence to frame him." Mom gave my hand a reassuring squeeze. "She seems confident she can get Rex off too if they can prove the cop's corruption."

Running my fingers through my tousled hair, I let out a shaky breath. The thought of Rex stuck in jail, possibly facing serious prison time, made my chest tighten with anxiety. He had risked everything to rescue me, to give me a second chance at life. I couldn't bear the idea of him suffering behind bars because of me.

"There's more," Mom continued. " Beau is staying behind in Portland to work with the lawyer on getting the guys out of jail. The rest of the club will be back today. Should be riding in within the next hour or two. They're bringing back a twelve-year-old girl and a woman in her twenties to the compound.

Beau said they were victims found in one of the shipping containers at the Moretti warehouse. The little girl's name is Aria. Beau said she seems to be really attached to the woman; Bree is her name."

My heart broke thinking of the horrors those poor souls must have endured.

"Oh my god. That's terrible."

Mom nodded solemnly.

"He warned they might be a bit skittish and will likely feel more comfortable around us women at first. Considering my past in the exact same situation and what you and Sarah have been through, I think we can really help them."

"Of course. We'll do whatever we can to help them feel safe here."

I told my mom I needed a few minutes to get ready. She nodded understandingly and left me to prepare myself.

Sliding out of bed, I changed out of my pajamas into a pair of comfy jeans and a soft t-shirt. I figured the poor girls would feel more at ease around someone who didn't look too put together. After tying my hair up into a messy bun, I quickly brushed my teeth and splashed some water on my face.

Staring at myself in the mirror, I couldn't help but reflect on how much progress I had made. The haunted hollowness in my eyes was gone, and there was a healthy flush to my cheeks. I owed so much to Rex, the Rebel Sons, and Sarah; they had given me a chance to live a real life.

Pushing those thoughts aside for now, I headed over to the clubhouse. Sarah and my mom were already there, along with Marlene and Cassandra, straightening up and making the space look warm and inviting.

"Hey," I greeted them with a soft smile. "What can I do to help get things ready?"

Sarah immediately pulled me into a hug.

"I'm so sorry about Rex," she murmured, her voice thick with empathy. "We'll get him out of this, I know it."

Blinking back tears, "we are just really good friends Sarah. I don't know why I feel so upset, I don't have the right to." Sarah gave my arm a comforting squeeze before releasing me.

"Anna, everyone but you two seem to know your more than just '*really good friends*'." She lifted her hands to make air quotes as she spoke.

The unmistakable rumble of bikes pulling into the compound make us all turn our heads. We all walked out to watch the guys pull in. They all pulled up in front of the clubhouse, followed by the club van that Park is driving.

Out of the back of the van comes Aria, a little girl with blonde hair. She's followed by Bree, a young woman in her twenties. Bree is beautiful, but the state she's in reminds me so much of how Rex found me in that basement. My heart breaks for them because I know all too well what these two have probably gone through before the Rebel Sons rescued them.

Aria clings tightly to Bree's hand, her big blue eyes wide with fear as she takes in her new surroundings. Bree's face is a canvas of fading bruises, her sunken eyes scanning the area warily. Despite her obvious apprehension, there's a protective fierceness in the way she holds the child close.

Sarah rushes over and crouches down in front of them, offering a warm smile. "Hi there, my name is Sarah. You're safe now, okay? These are my friends Anna, Sophia, Cassandra, and

Marlene." She gestures to each of us in turn.

Bree doesn't respond, simply tightening her grip on the little girl's hand. The Aria buries her face in Bree's side, peeking out at us cautiously.

"Why don't we get you two settled inside where it's comfortable?" Marlene speaks up, her grandmotherly presence seeming to put them at ease, if only slightly. "You've been through so much, but you don't have to be afraid anymore."

Slowly, Bree nods, and we guide them towards the clubhouse, the roar of the motorcycles fading into the background. As they pass by me, I can't help studying their appearances more closely. The little girl's shirt is stained and torn; her bare feet calloused. Bree is equally disheveled, her clothes hanging loosely on her slender frame.

My mind flashes back to those first few days after Rex rescued me - the constant state of hyper-vigilance, the way even the smallest noises made me flinch. I remember the overwhelming relief of finally feeling safe, yet still being haunted by the memories of my trauma.

I feel the panic attack coming on as I study the battered woman and little girl. Knowing it's going to happen; I excuse myself to the bathroom. I hurry as fast as I can, so no one sees what's about to happen. When I make it to the bathroom, I lock the door and slide my back down it until I'm sitting on the floor against the door.

I'm trying to get my breathing under control, but none of the techniques they showed me while I was in the hospital is helping. I feel like my airway is constricting. I can't breathe. Memories of being trapped in that room, the darkness, the fear. The feel of their hands on me. All the helplessness, it all comes flooding back in a tidal wave of anxiety.

My phone rings. I see the same number I saw yesterday and know it's Rex. With shaking hands, I answer the call, desperate for the sound of his voice to ground me.

It’s the same recording asking if I'll accept the charges. I manage to say yes but I can't get any more words out. Rex comes on the line; he must hear my erratic breathing.

"Anna? What's going on?" His deep voice is laced with concern knowing I'm not ok. It must finally click in place for him what is happening.

"Just breathe, baby. It's all going to be okay," Rex soothes, his gravelly tone somehow managing to penetrate the fog of panic clouding my mind. I try to focus on the sound of his voice, letting it anchor me.

"I... I can't..." I gasp out between ragged breaths. "I can feel it... them touching me."

"Listen to me, gorgeous. You're safe now, you hear me? Whatever you're seeing, whatever you're feeling, it can't hurt you anymore. I've got you. Even if I'm not there with you right now, I still got you. Always."

Rex's words slowly start to take hold, helping me regain control of my breathing bit by bit. The tightness in my chest begins to loosen as the memories lose their grip.

"That's it, nice and slow," he encourages. "You're doing so good, baby. Just keep breathing with me."

I match the rhythm of my inhales and exhales to the cadence of Rex's deep breaths filtering through the phone's speaker. The panic subsides, leaving me emotionally and physically drained but grounded once more.

"Thank you," I whisper shakily. "I don't know what happened. One minute I was fine, and the next..."

"Hey, no need to explain a damn thing, you hear me. You've been through hell. Panic attacks are gonna happen sometimes. I just wish I could hold you right now and make it all go away."

A sad smile tugs at the corner of my lips.

"Me too." I sigh softly. "But hearing your voice... it helped. You helped ground me."

"Always. I'll do whatever it takes to keep you steady and movin' forward. I hate being stuck in this shithole when you need me. You okay now?"

I take a deep, steadying breath before responding.

"I'm okay now, thanks to you. Just seeing that woman and little girl in such rough shape... it triggered some things, you know?"

Rex lets out a weary sigh.

"Shit, Anna... I didn't even think about that. I'm so sorry. You know I'd never want to put you through that if I could help it."

"I know, Rex. It's not your fault at all." I rake my fingers through my hair. "Those poor girls... they're going to need a lot of support and care to heal, both physically and mentally. We all will do whatever we can to help them feel safe here."

"That's my girl," Rex's gruff voice is tinged with pride. "Even after everything you went through, you're still so determined to help everyone else."

I can't help but smile at his words.

"Well, I had a pretty amazing example to follow with you guys taking me in and giving me a second chance."

There's a brief pause before Rex speaks again, his tone turning serious.

"Listen, I hate to cut this short, but I gotta go deal with some shit here real quick. I'll call you back soon as I can, okay?"

"Okay," I reply, feeling a slight pang of disappointment at having to end our conversation.

"Be safe."

"Always am. Talk to you later, gorgeous."

The call disconnects, and I slowly get to my feet, splashing some cool water on my face. Taking another few calming breaths, I steel my resolve before exiting the bathroom to rejoin the others.

Sarah immediately notices my slightly disheveled appearance and pulls me aside, concern etched on her features.

"Are you alright? I saw you rush off..."

I offer her a reassuring smile.

"I'm okay, just a bit shaken up seeing them in that condition. It brought back some... memories." I avoid going into too much detail, not wanting to burden Sarah with the full extent of my panic attack.

Understanding dawns in Sarah's eyes, and she gives my arm a gentle squeeze.

"I'm so sorry, Anna. I can't even imagine how difficult that must have been for you."

Shaking my head, I wave off her apology.

"Really, I'll be fine. My main concern right now is making sure those poor girls feel safe and cared for here. We need to do everything we can to help them start healing."

Sarah nods resolutely, "absolutely. They're in good hands here."

CHAPTER 19

Rex

I ended the call with Anna when I noticed across the room, three inmates were starting shit with X and Dom. The altercation started getting aggressive, exchanging shoves and heated words. In an instant, fists were flying.

"Back the fuck off!" I shouted, rushing over to back up my brothers.

As soon as I reached them, one of the inmates swung a wild haymaker at me. I ducked under his swing and drove my shoulder into his midsection, dropping him to the floor. Another inmate came at me from behind, but X had my back, tackling the guy to the ground.

Dom and the inmate I had knocked down were exchanging punches furiously. As I rushed towards them to help Dom, a loud alarm suddenly pierced through the air, signaling chaos in the cell block.

Guards came pouring in, batons drawn. "On the ground! Face down now!"

They had the numbers, so we complied, X, Dom, and I lying

flat as the guards swarmed over us. Metal cuffs were cinched brutally tight around our wrists as we were forced into submission. One guard planted his knee firmly between my shoulder blades.

"What's going on here?" a stern voice demanded. I craned my neck to see a stocky man in a sergeant's uniform glaring down at us.

"Just a little misunderstanding, Sarge," I grunted. "No need to..."

The air left my lungs as the guard drove his knee deeper into my back. "Can it, tough guy."

I'm trying to keep my anger in check as I am being escorted back to our cell block along with X, Dom, and the other inmates involved in the fight. I keep my head down, jaw clenched, as the guards roughly shove us forward.

The deafening noise of clanging chains and gruff commands reverberates down the grimy hallway. My hands are bound tightly behind me, the cold metal of the cuffs biting into my skin with each rough push from the guards.

We reach our cell block and the heavy metal door clangs open. The guard prods me in the back with his baton. "Keep moving, Riggs."

I stumble forward, "what the fuck, man? I'm supposed to be going back to my cell," I barked at the guard escorting me away from the others.

"Just keep walking." He orders.

I heard X yell out from behind me, "where the hell are you taking him?"

The guard ignored X's question, keeping a firm grip on my arm as he marched me down the hall towards the showers. This cannot be fucking good.

"Hey, I asked you a question! Where are you taking him?" X shouted again, the tone of his voice growing more urgent.

The guard remained silent as he marched me towards the shower area. When he tried shoving me through the door frame of the shower room, I planted my feet firmly and refused to budge. Despite his efforts, I was using my larger frame to resist his push. It was amusing watching him struggle against my weight, his face turning red with exertion.

"Get your ass in there, Riggs!" he snarls through gritted teeth, giving me another forceful shove.

Finally, I stumble over the threshold and into the dank, tiled room. As soon as I'm through the doorway, the guard slams the door shut behind me, the heavy clang of the lock engaging echoing off the walls.

My body tenses, ready for a fight, as I hear footsteps approaching from behind me. A figure steps out from the far corner of the room and into the light as they move closer. I am taken aback by how much this man looks like me. It's like looking in a fucking mirror, except for a few subtle differences. We lock eyes and stand mere inches apart from each other.

Not willing to leave anything up to chance, I attack before he can make the first move. He already has an advantage with my hands cuffed behind my back.

With my hands restrained, I am left with limited options. But I refuse to go down without a fight. Using all my strength, I propel my head forward and make solid contact with the fucker's nose. The sound of bone crunching echoes through the room as we both collapse to the floor, the force of my attack nearly knocking me unconscious. Despite the pain and disorientation, I feel a surge of satisfaction knowing that I have inflicted some damage.

“Goddamnit Rex! I’m not trying to fucking fight you! I just want to talk.” He wipes at the blood pouring from his nose with the back of his hand. “You broke my fucking nose,” he mutters. He slowly gets to his feet, then stumbles over to grab a towel to stem the bleeding.

"Who the fuck are you?"

The man fucking laughs. It deep, gruff tone echoes off the tiled walls.

"Well, Rex, that's a complicated question and an even more complicated answer. We only have three minutes."

I stared at him, still in shock at how much he resembles me.

"Then you better start talking and un-fucking-complicate it real quick."

"My name is Maverick," he starts. "I'm in this jail right now because I'm supposed to kill you with this shiv." He holds up a crude, prison-made weapon so I can see it.

He must see my body coil, ready to attack again, because he quickly holds his hands up and tosses the shiv to the other side of the room.

"Rex, I don't want to kill you. I volunteered for the job so I could have a chance to talk to you and make sure no one else killed you."

I scoff, "Oh yeah? And why the hell would you volunteer to kill someone, get yourself arrested, just to protect said person that you don't even know?"

Maverick sits down on the floor across from me.

"Because you're my brother, Rex. I know it's going to be hard to believe me, but it's true. I found out about six months back."

I stared at Maverick, skeptical of every word out of his mouth. The resemblance is uncanny, but his story seems too far-fetched to be true.

"You really expect me to believe you're my brother? Fan-fucking-tastic job to whoever found you and then sent you to fuck with me. You sure as shit do look a hell of a lot like me. But do you really think I would believe for a minute that my dad would have had a kid and not had anything to do with it? Ever?"

Maverick shakes his head, looking me dead in the eye.

"That's not what I'm saying at all. He didn't know, Rex. He has no fucking idea I even exist, just like you didn't know. Your mom was Elaine, right? Bailed on you and Beau before you even turned one?"

I nod slowly, feeling uneasy about how much he seems to know about my history. Maverick takes a deep breath before launching into his explanation.

"Elaine's my mom too. She was already pregnant with me when she left. She didn't know it at the time. By the time she found out it was too late to get rid of me and she was too ashamed to go back. She drifted around for a while, got mixed up with the wrong people. That's where my dad came into the picture, or who I was told was my dad. He's the president of the Hell's Hellions MC."

I stare at Maverick in disbelief as he reveals that my mother was involved with the Hell's Hellions MC president after leaving Beau and me behind and never looking back.

"Hatchet, the Prez of the Hellions, is your dad?" I ask incredulously. Maverick nods his confirmation.

"Yeah, and he's a sick son of a bitch. Mom was desperate, alone, and knocked up with me. She started hanging around the Hellions' clubhouse, trying to find someone to latch onto for protection. Hatchet took an interest in her and claimed her, his own little pregnant plaything."

My stomach churns at the thought of our mother being exploited by that vile piece of shit. Even if she was a worthless mother, no woman deserves that.

I've crossed paths with the Hellions a few times over the years, and they have a nasty reputation, even among outlaw MC's. To think my own blood brother, if he really is, was raised up in that shit pisses me off.

"So, what, she was just his little pregnant whore then?" I spit out. "She was basically a fucking kid. She would have only been 17 at the time."

"More or less. He kept her around the club and took care of our basic needs after she had me. As soon as she popped me out, he didn't want anything to do with her. She became a club whore. She must have been better at that than being a mother because they kept her around. We were both considered property of the Hellions.

Once I turned 16 Hatchet showed a little more interest in me. He made me prospect as soon as I turned 18. I was fully patched when I turned 19."

"Look, Maverick..." I begin, my tone softening somewhat. "I don't know what kind of twisted web the Hellions have spun to bring you in here, but I do know one thing..."

"It was Tony Moretti, Rex. He knew you were taking out Vincent Ruso. Knew you were following him; I don't know how. Moretti decided to let you go through with the hit. He planned it so you would get arrested afterward and someone would take you out inside," Maverick explains, his expression grave.

"What Tony didn't know is that the Rebel Sons were going to fuck up his entire organization. That was a big fucking surprise. When he had no men to send inside to take you out, he reached out to Hatchet."

I feel my blood boiling at the mention of that sadistic bastard Moretti trying to have me killed from behind bars. But the fact that he made a deal with the Hell's Hellions president pisses me off even more. Beau hadn't had the opportunity to tell us how strike day went down. Moretti making it out alive means Anna is still in danger.

"They have a history," Maverick continues. "Hatchet supplied Moretti guns and in return he supplied Hatchet drugs. When the Sons took out all the big players, most of the Moretti soldiers fled. He came to the Hellions looking for a man that could get the job done. Hatchet brought it to the club, and I volunteered."

I shake my head in disbelief, trying to process everything Maverick has revealed. Moretti was desperate enough to put a hit on me that he made a deal with Hatchet and the Hellions. And this man claiming to be my brother from that very same club volunteered to carry it out... just to talk to me?

"I don't know what kind of game you're playing at here, but you need to stop right now," I growl, my fists clenching instinctively. "If Moretti and Hatchet cooked this up to mess with me, you're barking up the wrong tree."

Maverick holds his hands up defensively.

"I'm not playing any games, Rex. You can choose to believe me or not, but I'm telling you the truth."

"Then what's the end game here Maverick? How do you see this playing out?" I ask, my voice tinged with skepticism.

Maverick lets out a deep sigh.

"I was thinking I could follow you guys back to Montana. Get a chance to know my family that I should have known my whole goddamn life." He shakes his head, running a hand through his shaggy hair.

"I wanted to give you and Beau the choice that was taken from all three of us." Maverick's shoulders slump in resignation. "You know what, fuck it, it doesn't matter anyway. As soon as I walk out of this jail... and you're alive, I'm a dead man because you're not."

I eye him warily, unsure if I can trust this man's motivations.

"Well, I'm not leaving anytime soon," I state flatly. "I'm in on a murder charge so if you want another go at it, just book another fucking stay."

"What evidence do they have on you?" Maverick asks.

I let out a humorless chuckle.

"Enough that if my lawyer can't spin it in my favor, I'm going to prison for the rest of my life." I shake my head, the weight of the situation bearing down on me.

Maverick's eyes narrow as he seems to think something over.

"I can make it go away," he says finally.

I raise a doubtful eyebrow. "Yeah? How's that?"

"We get you put in solitary. I'll call Hatchet and tell him I can't get to you because you're in the hole and I need you out in order to finish the job," Maverick explains. "I was only in here for an overnight. I'll go tonight to the county evidence locker and get the evidence they have on you. No evidence, no case, and you're a free man."

I stare at Maverick, considering his offer to make my case disappear. Part of me is cynical, wondering if this is some twisted plot to gain my trust before stabbing me in the back. But the other part of me wants to believe he's telling the truth about being my brother and that he genuinely wants to help. Having the evidence disappear would certainly help my case, but I can't shake the nagging feeling that this is too good to be true.

"I just need the case number, so I know what I'm looking for," Maverick adds, his expression earnest.

"You make it sound like breaking into a county evidence locker is an everyday fucking occurrence. You know they don't just leave the door open for anybody."

Maverick shoots me an annoyed look.

"I'm aware, dickhead. One of the Hellions fucks the cop that works security there on the night shift. I just got to go in while he has her distracted. We've done this before a few times for our boys, it's not a problem getting in and out."

Breaking into an evidence locker to make my case disappear seems risky as hell, but it would solve my problems.

"Alright, say I take you up on this offer. What's to stop you from just taking off once you have the evidence?"

Maverick shakes his head adamantly.

"I wouldn't do that, Rex. This is my chance to have an actual family, to get away from Hatchet and the Hellions' bullshit. I'm not about to fuck that up. I'm not one of them, I've never belonged there."

I study him, trying to gauge his sincerity. He does seem genuinely invested in this chance to connect with his supposed blood family. But can I really trust the word of a Hellion?

"Look, I get that you have no reason to trust me right now," Maverick says, seeming to read my mind. "But I put my life on the line here just to have the opportunity to meet you. Hatchet doesn't know I'm your brother, he thinks I'm just here to kill you for Moretti. If he finds out the truth..."

He trails off, not needing to explain further. We both know how unforgiving and vicious clubs can be when it comes to betrayal, real or perceived.

I let out a deep sigh, running a hand over my closely cropped hair.

"Alright, Maverick. I'll take the risk. But you better not fuck me over, you hear? The Hellions won't be the only MC out looking' to kill you if you do."

A relieved smile spreads across his face.

"You got my word, bro. I'll take care of everything."

Just then, the sound of keys jingling, and the lock of the door being turned echoes through the tiled room. The door opens and it's the guard that brought me in here. The door shuts behind him and Maverick directs his attention to the guard.

"Hey Ben, can you do me another favor and put him in solitary for the night?"

Ben glances between us uncertainly before giving a small nod.

"Yeah man, no problem. I'll be right back; I'll have to fill out an incident report so I have a reason to put him in the hole."

The guard leaves and I just stare at Maverick, unable to hide my apprehension any longer.

"You sure you can pull this off?"

He meets my gaze steadily.

"He's an old friend. He used to get beat up in school a lot until I made sure everyone left him alone. He owes me."

Maverick pulls a pen and a piece of paper out of his pocket. "I need your case number."

"You're really putting a lot on the line here, you know that?" I say gruffly, rattling off the case number Victoria had given me.

"I know, but like I said, this is my chance to have an actual family. To get away from Hatchet and the Hellions' bullshit once and for all."

The desperation in his voice rings true, and I find myself nodding slowly in understanding. I've seen enough guys get chewed up and spit out by that life to know how soul-crushing it can be.

"So, if I get you out of here, am I good to show up in Montana without getting shot?"

A ghost of a smile tugs at my lips. "Yeah, you come to the compound, and I'll take care of everything else. Introduce you to Beau, yeah? I'm trusting you on this. Don't make me regret it."

CHAPTER 20

Rex

The sound of the lock turning pulls me from my dark thoughts. The guard from the other day, Ben, steps in, a tray of food in his hands.

"Chow time, Riggs." He sets the tray down on the small metal table bolted to the floor, then turns to leave.

"Wait," I call out, my voice rough from disuse. "Any news on when I'm getting out of this hellhole?"

The guard pauses, glancing over his shoulder.

"Your lawyer is here now." He hesitates, then adds, "I should be taking you up soon to meet with her."

The door clangs shut, leaving me alone once more. I stare at the tray of food, my appetite nonexistent. Pushing it aside, I sink back down on the narrow bunk, burying my face in my hands.

All I can think about is Anna and Em. Are they safe? Is Emmalynn okay without me? I should be there, protecting them, not rotting in this goddamn cell.

A sudden flare of anger courses through me. If it wasn't for that fucking cop and Moretti, I wouldn't be in this mess. The urge to punch something nearly overwhelming.

But then the reminder of what's at stake sobers me, dousing the flames of my rage. I can't lose control, not when there are people counting on me. I have to keep it together and get the fuck outta here.

Letting out a heavy sigh, I lean back against the wall, staring up at the ceiling. The monotony of these four walls is slowly driving me insane. Four days. Four goddamn days alone in this tiny concrete box of a room. The walls feel like they're closing in, suffocating me with each passing hour. I can't take much more of this shit.

I pace back and forth, my strides limited by the confined space. There's nothing to do but think, and that's becoming more torturous by the minute. Memories and regrets swarm my mind like a plague of locusts, devouring any semblance of peace.

Rebecca's face floats before my eyes, her warm smile a cruel taunt. The image of her lifeless body after the crash plays on a hellish loop. The guilt still eats me alive after all this time. And then I fucked up even worse by shutting everyone out, even Emmalynn, the one piece of Beck I had left in this world. Dad and the guys had to step in, be the father I couldn't bring myself to be in the first few months after the accident.

I became a single father and a widower in the blink of a fucking eye. After that, I basically closed myself off to everyone because I'm too fucking afraid of losing anyone else. I couldn't handle that pain again. It damn near destroyed me the first time around.

So, I threw myself into work and being the dad Em deserved. Kept my circle small, just the club and my kid. I told myself that was enough, that I didn't need or want anything more in my life. I was just protecting myself; you know?

But then Anna came along and blew those walls I had built up around myself all to hell. I'm drawn to her in a way I can't fully explain or understand. She gets me, the parts of myself I keep locked away from the world. With her, I don't have to pretend to be the tough, unshakable man. I can just... be.

Part of me wants nothing more than to pull her into my arms and never let go. To keep her safe, protect her from any more hurt or pain. To maybe, finally, open myself up again after all this time. But then the fear comes crashing back. What if something happens and I lose her? I don't know if I'm strong enough to survive that a second time. Fuck, I'm not even sure I really survived it the first time around.

So, I keep her at an arm's length, as much as it kills me. I bury my feelings deep down where I don't have to face them. It's a coward's move, but it's the only way I know how to guard myself. Because the truth is, I'm terrified of taking that risk, of fully letting someone in again, only for them to be ripped away. I'm scared shitless of that devastation, that all-consuming void of emptiness and loss.

I sink down onto the bunk, my head in my hands. What the hell is wrong with me? Anna went through unimaginable trauma and I'm over here wallowing in self-pity like a little bitch.

Gritting my teeth, I force myself to my feet again. I can't keep going down these dark paths, I have to keep fighting, have to get out of this shithole.

Victoria said she's working on getting the charges dropped, but it's gonna take time. I don't have time. Not with Moretti still gunning for us and dragging the Hellions into it.

The lock on the door sounds again, the same guard Ben opens the heavy metal door.

"Come on Riggs, your lawyer is waiting to talk to you."

Ben escorts me down the familiar corridor to the same private interview room we were in before. When we enter, it's just Victoria seated at the table, her fiery red hair cascading over one shoulder as she looks up from the stack of files before her. I let out a sigh of relief that my dad isn't here.

"Thanks, Ben," Victoria dismisses the guard before turning her piercing green eyes on me.

"Have a seat, Rex."

I lower myself into the cold metal chair across from her, the cuffs on my wrists clinking against the table. Her gaze roams over me appraisingly for a moment before she speaks.

"You look like shit." The blunt observation is punctuated by the faintest hint of a smirk playing at the corners of her full lips.

I huff out a humorless chuckle, shaking my head.

"Yeah, well, you try getting a good night's sleep in this fucking place."

Her expression softens a fraction.

"I'm working on getting you and the others out. But it's not going to be easy in your case."

Leaning back in the chair, I fix her with a pointed look.

"Just give it to me straight, Red. What are we looking at here?"

Victoria purses those lips briefly before diving in.

"The cop who arrested you, Jameson, is a piece of work. Has a history of excessive force complaints, witness intimidation allegations. I've got a few ideas on how we can discredit him."

"Red, I'm not sure what lawyer shit you gotta do but you need to file something that would make them look over what evidence they have on me."

Victoria nods. "I will be soon; I have to file a motion of discovery."

"No, Red, you need to do it as soon as you leave here." I fix her with a hard stare.

"Rex, what aren't you telling me?"

I take a deep breath, running a hand over my close-cropped hair.

"There was a guy in here, he said his name is Maverick. The guy looks just like me, like freaky Friday type shit." I shake my head, still unable to wrap my mind around it.

"He said he's my brother. Beau and I never knew about him."

Victoria's eyes widen fractionally, but she stays silent, clearly waiting for me to continue.

"He said he was going to break into the county evidence locker and take the evidence they have on me. If he's true to his word, it's already done."

Her fingers are already flying over her phone, typing out a text, no doubt trying to get ahead of this latest development. After a few moments, she looks back up at me.

"Who is this Maverick's mother supposed to be?"

"Elaine Riggs," I reply grimly.

She nods slowly, taking that in as her thumbs continue tapping out messages.

"How old would he be? You're 35, correct?"

"Yeah. He said our mom found out she was pregnant with him after she left us right before I turned one. So, 33?"

Victoria's phone vibrates and she glances down at the message, her eyes widening slightly as she reads it. After a moment, she looks back up at me, her expression unreadable.

"Well, it seems your mysterious 'brother' was telling the truth. There was a certificate of birth issued in Oregon for a Maverick Thomas Riggs, with the mother listed as Elaine Riggs. She was seventeen at the time and no father is named on the certificate."

I feel like the wind has been knocked out of me as the confirmation sinks in. A brother, a blood relative I never knew existed until now. How is that even possible? All the questions and doubts swirling through my mind must be evident on my face.

Victoria's voice pulls me from my daze.

"Rex, I need you to focus here. We can dig into the details of this later, but right now we have to deal with the matter at hand." Her tone is firm but not unkind.

"If what you're saying is true, and this Maverick is going to tamper with evidence, that's going to open up a whole new can of worms."

I nod slowly, forcing myself to concentrate despite the million-mile-an-hour thoughts racing through my brain.

"Yeah, I get it. Just tell me what you need me to do."

"For now, nothing. I'll have to move quickly and get the proper motions filed to get all the evidence against you disclosed and reviewed by an impartial third party."

Her fingers are flying over her phone again as she speaks.

"That should reveal if anything has been compromised and give me an angle to attack from. I'm having one of my associates start the paperwork now. It will be filed with the court within the hour. I'll let you know as soon as I hear anything."

"Thanks." I stand up and head towards the door so the guard can escort me out. I turn back around just as Ben is unlocking the door.

"Hey Red, don't say anything to my dad about Maverick. I want to be the one to tell him. That kind of news is going to devastate him."

Victoria nods, "absolutely Rex, it should come from you."

* * *

Ben was escorting me back to my cell when the three guys that had jumped X and Dom the day after we got here come around the corner.

"Get back to your cells," Ben said forcefully as he reached for his baton. It's then I noticed the Hellions tat on the side of the smallest guy's neck. *Fuck*.

All three of them came at Ben and me. The biggest fucker charged right at me. I tried to sidestep his rush, but the confined space worked against me. His shoulder slammed into my gut, driving the air from my lungs as I was shoved back against the concrete wall.

Before I could recover, meaty fists were raining down blows on my face and torso. I tasted copper as my lip split open. Spots danced in my vision from a vicious shot that caught me square in the eye socket.

Rage erupted within me, and I lowered my shoulder, driving into the big guy's midsection like a battering ram. He grunted and stumbled back a step. Using the momentum, I whipped my cuffed hands up and around, catching him in the throat with the chain.

The big bastard gurgled and went down clutching at his crushed windpipe. As he crumpled to the floor, I spun to face the other two Hellion assholes.

One was down on the ground, Ben's baton a blur as he mercilessly worked the piece of shit over. But the third was circling behind Ben with his back to me, a shiv made from a rusted piece of metal clutched in his fist.

Just as he was about to stab Ben, I put my cuffed hands over his head and jerked him back by his neck, the chain of the cuffs digging into his throat. He let out a strangled gasp as I cut off his air supply.

The inmate thrashed and flailed, trying to break free of my choke hold. I tightened my grip, pouring every ounce of strength into squeezing the life out of this piece of shit. His face turned a deep purple, bulging veins protruding from his forehead and neck as he struggled for breath.

He lashed out blindly, his elbow slamming into my ribs with a sickening crack. White hot pain lanced through my side, but I refused to let up. Through gritted teeth, I wrenched the chain tighter, shutting out the pain radiating through my body.

The inmate's movements became more feeble, his fight draining away with each passing second. Just when I thought he was about to go limp, he drove the shiv deep into my thigh.

A guttural roar tore from my throat as burning pain erupted in my leg. Blinding fury washed over me, and I yanked back on the chain with every ounce of strength left in me. His airway was completely severed, his eyes bulging grotesquely as he choked and sputtered.

He tried to pry at the chain digging into his neck, but his struggles were rapidly fading. With one final violent convulsion, the life left his body and he collapsed into a heap on the floor, eyes frozen wide in a glassy, dead stare.

I shoved the lifeless corpse off of me, a tremor of rage and revulsion passing through me. Gulping in ragged breaths, my gaze landing on Ben.

The guard was slumped against the wall, out of breath but alive.

"Is your leg bad?" He managed to gasp out between breaths.

I grit my teeth against the searing pain radiating from the stab wound in my thigh.

"Just a flesh wound," I respond, forcing the words out through clenched jaws.

Ben drags himself to his feet, favoring his left side where one of the Hellions must have gotten a few good licks in. He limps over and crouches down next to me, eyeing the makeshift shiv still embedded in my leg.

"Good, you need to get the hell out of here and get back to your cell block before they pin another murder charge on you. I'll take care of all this; I'll tell them it was me who did this. They jumped me, you helped get them off me."

I start to protest, but Ben cuts me off with a sharp shake of his head.

"Don't argue with me, Riggs. Just get your ass back to gen pop before the cavalry arrives."

Nodding reluctantly, I force myself to my feet, putting as little weight as possible on my injured leg. Ben grabs the shiv, grimacing as he pulls it free. A fresh gush of blood immediately soaks through the fabric of my prison-issue pants.

"Get going," Ben growls, ripping a strip of cloth from his own shirt to bind the wound. "I've got your back on this one."

With a final nod of gratitude, I turn and limp back towards the main cell block, leaving Ben to clean up the mess. My mind is racing, trying to process everything that's happened.

"Hey Riggs..." Ben yells to get my attention from behind my back. I pause in the corridor, leaning against the wall as a wave of dizziness washes over me. Blood loss and adrenaline are taking their toll. I turn to look at the guard.

"Thank you."

I give Ben a curt nod in response, then turn and continue my slow, agonizing journey back towards gen pop. Each step sends a fresh jolt of fiery pain lancing up my leg, but I grit my teeth and push forward.

Rounding the corner, I spot two guards up ahead arguing over something. One of them glances over and does a double take when he sees me approaching, covered in blood and favoring my injured leg.

"Riggs! What the hell is going on?" The guard rushes over, his partner right behind him with his hand resting on the butt of his sidearm. I raise my cuffed hands in a placating gesture.

"Easy, fellas. I was just in a little... disagreement. Nothing I couldn't handle."

The guards exchange a skeptical look, their eyes roving over my battered appearance and the trail of blood I'm leaving in my wake. The second guard's hand tightens on his gun grip.

"Where's Ben? He was supposed to be escorting you back to your cell."

I jerk my head back the way I came.

"He's back there cleaning up his mess. Got a little hairy for a minute, but he'll fill you in." I force a pained grin. "I gotta get this leg looked at."

The first guard eyes me warily for a beat, then nods.

"Alright, let's get you to the infirmary. But we're gonna have to put you in solitary after that until we get to the bottom of this shit."

Suppressing a groan, I nod my agreement. As much as I hate being locked down in solitary, right now it's better than staying in gen pop and having to constantly watch my back. At least in the hole I'll be able to get some damn rest without worrying about being shanked in my sleep.

With the guards taking up positions on either side of me, I allow them to escort me towards the jail's medical wing. Each labored step is pure torture, the makeshift bandage on my thigh already soaked through with blood. I feel lightheaded and nauseous, but I lock my jaw and push those sensations down, focusing on putting one foot in front of the other.

As we near the infirmary, a small smile tugs at the corners of my mouth. Despite the shitstorm this day has turned into, at least I was able to take out a few Moretti's hired Hellion bitches. A tiny sliver of satisfaction amidst all the chaos. I'll take whatever wins I can get right now. Because this war is just getting started.

CHAPTER 21

Anna

"Anna, when is daddy going to come home? I miss him and grandpa," Emmalynn asks, her big blue eyes pooling with unshed tears as she gazes up at me imploringly.

The sadness etched on her tiny cherub face is utterly heartbreaking. It's been almost three weeks since she has seen Rex. My heart clenches in my chest as I pull her into a tight embrace, her small frame trembling against me. How do I explain the harsh realities of the situation to this innocent child? I don't have the answers she desperately seeks.

"I don't know, sweetie," I murmur, my voice thick with emotion as I stroke her silky brown curls. "But I promise you, your daddy and grandpa are doing everything they can to come back to you as soon as possible."

Emmalynn sniffles, burying her face in the crook of my neck. No child should ever have to endure such fear and uncertainty. I tighten my arms around her, rocking us gently back and forth as I fight back my own tears.

"Your daddy is the strongest, bravest man I've ever known," I assure her, hoping my words offer some semblance of comfort.

"And your grandpa would move heaven and earth to keep your daddy and you, safe. They'll be home before you know it."

But even as the reassuring words leave my lips, doubt gnaws at the back of my mind. No one else in the club seems to have any concrete answers either. The silence surrounding Rex, Beau, and the others' situation is deafening, fueling the anxiety that threatens to consume me.

All I can do is hold Emmalynn close, silently praying that the men we love return to us unharmed, and that this nightmare ends soon. Her unwavering faith in her father's invincibility is both inspiring and heartbreaking. I only hope I can muster that same strength to keep us both afloat until they come home.

"Em, daddy is working really hard on getting home to you, I promise. I'll call grandpa while you're at school and I'll let him know you're missing him so he can call you after you get home, deal?"

Emmalynn nods solemnly, her lower lip trembling as she fights to be brave.

"And daddy will call too?"

"I'm not sure, sweetheart. I'll try." I force a reassuring smile, gently wiping away a stray tear that rolls down her rosy cheek.

"Your daddy loves you more than anything in this world. He'll move mountains to talk to his best girl if he is able to. Where daddy is working, he can't have his cell phone. That makes it really hard for him to call. He's really trying though Em, promise."

"Okay," she murmurs, her shoulders relaxing slightly as she leans into my embrace.

"I love you, Anna."

Those four simple words pierce straight through to my battered soul, filling the cracks and fissures that have formed from a lifetime of heartache.

"I love you too, Em. So much."

I notice movement out of the corner of my eye at my open office door. It's Jake, Wyatt, and Gunnar.

A flush of heat creeps up my neck as I wonder how long they've been standing there, unnoticed. Have they overheard my attempts to soothe Emmalynn's fears? The thought makes me self-conscious.

Jake's expression is unreadable, his chiseled features a stoic mask as he meets my gaze. Wyatt, however, looks visibly shaken, his eyes clouded with worry. Gunnar's brow is creased, his thick arms folded across his broad chest.

I open my mouth to greet them, but the words catch in my throat. An awkward silence stretches between us, thick with unspoken questions and concerns. Finally, Jake clears his throat.

"Everything alright in here?" His deep voice is a low rumble, laced with a protective edge.

I nod, forcing a tight smile as I gently disentangle myself from Emmalynn's embrace.

"Yeah, we're okay. Em was just missing her dad and grandpa."

Em immediately perks up at the presence of her "uncles", her childlike exuberance returning in an instant.

Wyatt strides into the cramped office space, his towering frame seeming to fill the room with his easygoing energy. Em's face lights up like a Christmas tree as he approaches, her previous worries forgotten for the moment.

"Hey cutie, it's my turn to take you to school," Wyatt says, flashing that signature lopsided grin of his. "You ready to go?"

"Yeah, Uncle Wy, I'm ready," Em chirps, bouncing on the balls of her feet with barely contained excitement. Her eyes flit to the stuffed unicorn backpack on the sofa.

"Will you carry my backpack? It's heavy."

Wyatt smirks in response. His relaxed demeanor somehow putting me more at ease.

"I think I can handle that."

He crosses the room in a few long strides, easily scooping up the bag with one hand. The shimmering pinks and purples of the unicorn design seem comically out of place, slung over Wyatt's shoulder against his kutte and club colors. He handles it with an effortless cool, as if toting around a sparkling purple and pink unicorn backpack is just another day in the life.

"Goddamn, this is heavy. What did Gram pack in your lunch Em, rocks?" Wyatt jokes, hoisting the unicorn backpack higher onto his broad shoulders.

Em gets a serious look on her face, her face pinched in that adorably stern way only a five-year-old can manage.

"I don't know Uncle Wy, but you better check because if she did you need to stop and get me lunch, and you're paying."

A surprised laugh bubbles up from deep within me at her serious tone. Leave it to Emmalynn to keep Wyatt on his toes. He feigns an affronted gasp, clutching at his chest dramatically.

"Princess! You're questioning Gram's legendary lunch-packing skills?" He shakes his head in mock disappointment.

"For that, I'm making you buy me ice cream later as penance."

Em giggles, her earlier worries forgotten as she banters back and forth with her beloved uncle. The weight of the last few days seems to lift ever so slightly from my shoulders as I watch their playful exchange. In these stolen moments of light-heartedness, it's almost possible to forget the turmoil swirling around us.

Wyatt holds out his hand expectantly.

"C'mon squirt, let's get you to school before your teacher has my head."

Em's eyes light up and she eagerly takes his outstretched hand, her tiny fingers dwarfed by his much larger ones. As they turn to leave, she glances back over her shoulder at me.

"Uncle Wy thinks Miss Olivia is a smoke show," Emmalynn pipes up innocently.

Gunnar lets out a booming laugh that seems to shake the very walls of my cramped office. I shoot him a withering glare, but it only seems to spur his amusement further.

Jake tries and fails to hide his own snicker, shaking his head in faux disapproval.

"Didn't I tell you to watch what you say around her? Little ears have big mouths Wyatt."

Wyatt's face turns an impressive shade of red.

"Em where did you hear that?"

She shrugs nonchalantly. "I heard you say it when you dropped me off last. You told Uncle Talon that Miss Olivia was a real smoke show."

Wyatt groans, pinching the bridge of his nose.

"Ah, kid. You're not supposed to repeat everything you hear, remember?"

"But Uncle Wy, you're the one who said..."

"I know, I know, it's my fault." He holds up a hand to silence her protests. "Just... don't say that again, okay?"

"So, I shouldn't tell Miss Olivia that you think she's a smoke show?"

“Noooo!" All four of us reply in unison.

"Keeping that in all day will be hard work Uncle Wy. You will have to buy me ice cream for your penance when you pick me up from school today."

I try to hide my laughter behind my hand as Em bargains with Wyatt, her eyes sparkling with mischief.

"Em, you little hustler. If you keep this up, Uncle Wy is going to be broke before you hit middle school."

Wyatt shakes his head in mock exasperation, but the corners of his lips twitch with amusement.

"Yeah, kid. Ice cream it is. Just this once, deal?"

Em taps her chin, pretending to mull it over for a moment before nodding solemnly.

"It's a deal if I get whipped cream and sprinkles too."

Jake clears his throat.

"Alright, you two troublemakers better get going before you're late."

"We're going," Wyatt shoots his brother a lopsided grin. He holds out his hand for Emmalynn once more.

"C'mon short stack, let's roll."

She beams up at him, easily falling back into her usual sunny disposition as she takes his hand. As they turn to leave, Emmalynn glances back at me over her shoulder.

"Bye Anna! I'll see you after school!"

"Bye sweetie," I murmur, unable to keep the affectionate smile from tugging at my lips. "Have a good day."

I watch as Emmalynn stops just before leaving with Wyatt, throwing her little arms around Jake and Gunnar's necks to hug them both at once. Her tiny frame is dwarfed between their towering, muscular builds.

She whispers something, her words too soft for me to make out, but judging by the amused grins that spread across Jake and Gunnar's faces, I can only imagine what sort of mischievous remark just left her lips.

As Wyatt guides her out, her footsteps fading away along with the echoes of her infectious laughter, Jake and Gunnar exchange a look. A deep belly laugh rumbles up from Gunnar's broad chest, the sound rich and booming.

"She said she already told Miss Olivia last week," he chuckles, shaking his head in bemused disbelief.

Jake remarks, "Doesn't she act exactly like Rex?"

"Miss Olivia, huh? Can't say I blame him."

"She's too young for you, old man." I remark in a playful tone, a small smile playing on my lips. In that moment, it's easy to forget the darkness looming over us all. Emmalynn has a way of injecting light and laughter into even the bleakest of situations.

The smiles slip from Jake and Gunnar's faces, replaced by tense expressions. Reality comes crashing back in harsh waves.

Jake clears his throat, his stormy gaze locking with mine.

"We need to talk, Anna."

The gravity of Jake's words hangs heavy in the air. My heart skips a beat as dread coils in the pit of my stomach. I nod slowly, forcing myself to meet his piercing gaze.

"Okay. What's going on?"

Jake exchanges a weighted look with Gunnar before turning back to me.

"We got a call from Beau earlier this morning."

I brace myself for whatever bomb he's about to drop. Has something happened to Rex? Or the others? A million worst-case scenarios race through my mind in those agonizing seconds of silence.

"They were able to get X and Dom released on bail, Beau will have them out by the end of the day." Jake continues gruffly.

"But Rex..."

He trails off, his jaw tensing as he seems to struggle to find the right words. Gunnar steps forward, his expression solemn.

"Rex's situation is more complicated. The lawyer thinks she can get the charges dropped eventually, but it's going to be another day or two before he gets out."

My chest tightens as Gunnar’s words sinks in. Another day or two...

"Wait, another day or two? Is Rex getting out?" I demand, desperation creeping into my voice.

Jake nods, a smile slowly stretching across his handsome face.

"Yeah, he's a lucky bastard. The lawyer filed something asking for them to produce what evidence they had on Rex, and they couldn't find it. No evidence, no case."

I let out the breath I didn't even realize I was holding, the tension seeping from my body as relief washes over me. Rex is getting out. Those three words play on a loop in my mind, a soothing mantra that steadies my racing heart.

"Oh, thank God," I murmur, sinking back into the worn sofa cushions as my legs suddenly feel like jelly. Tears of relief prick at the corners of my eyes, but I blink them back furiously.

"When will he be released exactly?"

Gunnar shrugs one broad shoulder.

"Could be later today, could be tomorrow, or next week. We just don’t know. Beau's working on getting the bail situation sorted as we speak."

I nod slowly, processing this information. Rex will be home soon. Back with Emmalynn. Back with me. A tiny flutter stirs in my chest at that thought, one I quickly tamp down. Now is not the time.

"Anna." Jake's deep voice cuts through my thoughts, his tone laced with a strange urgency. I glance up, taken aback by the intensity burning in his stormy eyes.

"There's something else you need to know."

I tense instinctively, bracing myself for another bout of bad news. "What is it?"

Jake seems to hesitate for a moment before pressing on.

"When they get back, things are going to be... complicated. For all of us."

A crease forms between my brows as confusion swirls within me.

"What do you mean?"

"While they were in county lock-up, a rival club was brought into the jail. Things got heated between our guys and this other club."

My stomach drops as the implications of his words sink in like a lead weight.

"Oh no. Were they hurt? Rex, is he..."

"He's okay, more or less," Jake reassures me quickly, holding up a hand to stop my spiral.

"But let's just say your dad and the other club didn't take too kindly to Moretti getting what was coming to him and all his players."

I feel my cheeks flush with a mixture of shame and anger.

"I'm so sorry I brought all this on you guys. How bad is it going to get for you guys?" I ask, my voice barely above a whisper.

The two men exchange another weighted look, their expressions grim.

"We're not sure yet," Gunnar admits. "But if things escalate with this rival club like we think they might... it will get ugly."

.

Jake comes and sits beside me on the couch. His intense gaze burns into me as he leans forward, elbows resting on his knees.

"Anna, look at me."

I slowly raise my head to meet his eyes, my heart thundering in my chest. The weight of guilt and shame is a lead ball in the pit of my stomach.

Jake's expression softens as he holds my stare.

"You didn't bring any of this on the club, on Rex, on any of us," he states firmly.

"We were already in the middle of it when we found you."

His words are like a balm, soothing some of the anguish clawing at my insides. Still, I can't shake the nagging sense of responsibility that plagues me.

"I am more grateful to you than anyone else on this earth, sweetheart," Jake continues, his voice taking on a gruff tenderness.

"If it wasn't for you, I wouldn't have Sarah or my son."

My breath catches in my throat at the raw emotion flickering in his stormy eyes.

"I owe my whole life to you," he murmurs. "And we saved a lot of girls in those shipping containers from a world of hurt and heartache because of you and the intel you gave us."

Jake leans back, shaking his head slowly.

"We couldn't have done any of that without you."

His gaze bores into me with an intensity that seems to pierce my very soul.

"So just stop with all that 'I'm sorry' bullshit because there isn't a damn one of the brothers that's sorry you're here," he states, his deep voice leaving no room for argument. "You got me?"

I'm at a loss for words, overcome with emotion. The only thing I can think to do is hug him. I nearly launch myself at Jake and hug him as hard as I can.

Caught off guard, it takes Jake a moment to hug me back.

"You good?" he asks me softly.

"Yeah," I reply, my voice thick with emotion.

"I just realized I'm hugging a man and I'm not scared. Rex has been the only man that hasn't scared me since you guys found me."

"That's real good, sweetheart," Jake murmurs, the rumble of his voice soothing against my ear. "I'm glad you're not scared, but if Sarah walked in here, I'm not sure what she'd think of me huggin' another woman this long on a couch."

I let out a watery laugh, tightening my embrace.

"She's really got you by the balls, huh? She's my sister, which makes you my brother. She'll get over it. Besides, you're surprisingly cuddly despite all the muscle. She should share. This is like therapy."

Jake's deep laugh reverberates through his broad chest. I squeeze him tightly one more time.

"Thank you, Jake."

"Anytime," he replies as I finally pull away, offering me a lopsided smile.

"What happens next," I ask.

"We'll handle it, one way or another," Jake states, his tone brooking no argument.

"Our priority is getting our brothers back home safe, then we lock this place down and figure out our next moves."

I can only nod mutely, my mind whirling. Just when the darkness is lifting, another storm is already brewing on the horizon, this one more ominous and menacing than the last.

But as I meet Jake's resolute stare, I find strength in the determination blazing in his eyes. These men, my newfound family, will do whatever it takes to protect what's theirs. Gratitude and affection for them washes over me, steadying my resolve. If a war is coming, I'll be ready to face it beside them, come what may.

Rex is coming home. That's all that matters right now.

CHAPTER 22

Rex

The road blurs beneath my wheels as I push the limits, my bike growling with each twist of the throttle. Jake and X flank me, with my dad leading our way. Jett, Talon, Patch, and Dom ride behind us. Our formation tight as we tear through the winding backroads. The compound can't come into view soon enough. We have about 10 miles left until we are home.

I spent nearly another week in solitary waiting on any news from Victoria on my case. When she came back in two days ago saying the evidence had been "misplaced", I'd never been more thankful in my life.

All charges against X and Dom have been dropped. With my case being a little more complicated, mine hasn't officially been dropped but I was free to go. I was told to stay in Oregon but fuck that. I was coming home to my daughter, to my woman.

With each mile marker passed, I grow more anxious to see Em's bright smile again. How many nights did I lie awake, haunted by the memory of her voice asking when I'd be home? Too damn many. But that torture is over now.

Walking out of the jail I expected to see Maverick or the Hellions waiting for me. There was no one but my brothers, my family. Jake, Jett, Talon, and Patch rode back to Oregon to make the ride back home with us. We expected the Hellions to be waiting but so far, it's been a quiet ride.

The compound's gates finally come into view, and I feel the knot in my chest loosen. I'm home. As we roll through the compound, pulling up to the clubhouse, I catch sight of familiar faces, brothers and families alike.

But it's the blur of dark pigtails that has me damn near leaving my bike before it's stopped. Em sprints towards me, her little legs carrying her as fast as they can.

"Daddy!" she cries out, slamming into my arms as I scoop her up, pulling her close.

"Hey, baby girl," I murmur into her hair. I'm never letting her go again. "I missed you so much. I'm so sorry I was gone so long."

I hold Em tight, savoring the moment of finally being reunited with her after what felt like an eternity away. Her familiar scent and the warmth of her little body against mine grounds me, reminding me of what truly matters.

"I missed you too, daddy," her tears wetting my neck, her voice muffled but filled with relief. "Don't ever leave me again."

The guilt hits me square in the chest at her innocent plea.

"Never again, baby girl. I never wanted to be away from you for so long." I pull back slightly to look into her eyes, gently brushing a stray curl from her face. "But I promise, I'm not going to be away from you that long anymore. Not ever."

The sound of footsteps approaching catches my attention, and I look up to see Anna making her way towards us. My breath catches in my throat at the sight of her. I swear she's even more beautiful than I remember. Her dark chocolate eyes lock with mine, a mixture of emotions flickering across her face.

"Hey," she breathes out, coming to a stop in front of us. "You're back."

"Yeah, I'm back," I reply, my voice thick with unspoken feelings. Em wiggles out of my arms and I set her down, unable to tear my gaze away from Anna.

My dad comes up behind me and I realize Em was wiggling out of my hold on her to get to her grandpa. She's never been away from either of us this long since she's been born. The distance was hard on both of them. Dad's been there being another dad to Em since Rebecca died. All my brothers have, but especially my dad.

"Grandpa!" Em yells as she launches herself at him. He scoops her up, tossing her in the air and catching her with a boisterous laugh.

"There is grandpa's little princess!" Dad's eyes crinkle with pure joy as he peppers Em's face with kisses, eliciting a fit of giggles from her. "Did you keep everyone in line for me while I was gone?"

"Uh huh, you know it!" Em nods emphatically.

Anna's watching the exchange with a soft smile, her eyes shining with an emotion I can't quite place. When our eyes meet, I feel that familiar pull to her that's always there with her.

"Rex." Dad's gruff voice pulls me back. He's studying me intently, still cradling Em in his arms.

"We got church. Back at the clubhouse in an hour."

I give a slight nod in understanding. "Sure, Prez. I'm gonna spend some time with Em and grab a shower. I'll be here in an hour."

Satisfied, he turns his attention back to Em, tickling her sides as she squeals in delight. I can't help but grin at their easy affection, happy to have my family back together.

"I'm going to head back over to work in the office. I'm really glad you're home, Rex." Anna states as she starts to walk past me. I gently grab her forearm to stop her, being careful not to scare her.

"Hey," I wait until she meets my gaze. "I'm gonna spend some time with Em and take care of what I need to, and then I'll see you later."

Her eyes search mine for a moment, and I can see the slight tension leave her shoulders. A small smile tugs at the corners of her mouth as she gives a barely perceptible nod. Without another word, she turns and continues towards the garage where our semi fleet is housed.

I watch her retreating form for a few seconds before Em's delighted squeal pulls me back. Turning, I see dad has her upside down, her pigtails nearly brushing the ground as she laughs uncontrollably.

"Alright, you two," I chuckle, unable to wipe the grin off my face. "Em, come tell me everything I've missed since I've been gone."

Setting Em back on her feet, dad ruffles her hair affectionately.

"You heard your old man. Go see your dad for a bit. I'll be over later to see you."

Em beams up at me, her whole face alight with happiness.

"Okay! Come on, daddy, let's go!"

She grabs my hand and tugs me eagerly towards my house, and I can't resist scooping her up and tossing her over my shoulder. Her squeals of laughter are like music to my ears as I carry her. I'm so damn happy to finally see my girl again, both of them.

* * *

An hour later, we're all gathered around the table in the chapel. The familiar scent of leather and whiskey hangs in the air, a comforting reminder that I'm back home with my brothers. As dad settles into his chair at the head of the table, his demeanor immediately demands the attention from all those around him.

"First off, I want to thank all of you for keeping shit together while Rex and I were dealing with that mess up in Portland," he begins, his gravelly voice echoing in the room. "Couldn't have done it without each and every one of you stepping up."

A chorus of murmurs and nods ripple through the room, the bonds of brotherhood evident in the way we all rally behind dad's words. His gaze settles on Gunnar and Jax, a silent cue for them to take the lead.

Jax clears his throat, his fingers flying across the keyboard of his laptop as he pulls up various files and schematics.

"Alright, let's run through the tactical side of strike day first." He proceeds to walk us through each location we hit.

"The only team that was unsuccessful was the members sent from Rocky Mount and Hazard. They couldn't get to Moretti in time to take him out before he fled. His mansion in Jersey had an underground tunnel system. He escaped our men through the tunnels as soon as we gained access to his property. They did recover a large amount of cash."

As Jax wraps up, Gunnar takes over, his gruff demeanor a stark contrast to Jax's youthful exuberance.

"Now for the financial rundown..." He launches into a comprehensive breakdown of the assets seized, cash recovered, and financial blows dealt to the Moretti organization.

The numbers are staggering, and a sense of pride swells within me as I listen to the extent of the damage we inflicted. Gunnar's report is a testament to the precision and coordination of our efforts, a well orchestrated assault on the Moretti empire's lifeblood.

"Which brings us to a total of over twenty-five million in liquid assets recovered, not to mention the countless businesses and revenue streams we've effectively crippled."

A low whistle escapes from someone's lips, but the sentiment is shared by all of us. We dealt a devastating blow, one that will take Moretti years to recover from, if ever.

"Anna has been working on moving the cash around and ways to clean it for us. It's going to take us awhile; we didn't plan on there being so much cash hidden in those businesses." Gunnar concludes, his steely gaze sweeping across the room.

Dad nods, a slight smile tugging at the corners of his mouth.

"Nicely done, boys. We're not letting up until that bastard is put down for good. Gunnar, I want you to start looking at different businesses for sale around our area and each chapter. I think the best way to use that money is to invest it back into the club."

A chorus of affirmative grunts and murmurs fills the room, the determination and resolve palpable. Dad then directs his attention to me.

"VP, fill the boys in on the information you came across in county."

I lean back in my chair, taking a deep breath as the weight of the situation settles over me. All eyes are on me, waiting for me to share the details of what went down in that county lockup. I begin, my voice low and measured.

"Things got a little heated back in Portland when we first got hauled in." I recount the scuffle X and Dom found themselves in with three of the Hellions right off the bat.

"Dumb fucks didn't know who they were messing with," I say with a humorless chuckle.

"Should've left well enough alone." I take a deep breath, steeling myself for what I'm about to reveal.

"After the fight with the Hellions in county, one of the guards pulled me aside, separating me from X and Dom."

The room falls deathly silent, every eye fixed on me as I recount the chilling encounter.

"Turns out Moretti is working with the Hellions now that he's got none of his crew left standing or breathing. He sent those three pricks into county to try and take me out."

A low rumble of anger ripples through the gathered men, their loyalty and protectiveness towards me palpable.

"They came after me again, but I took them all out with the help of that guard. He took the heat for it; said he was the one to finish them off for attacking both of us."

Jett, shaking his head in disbelief. "Moretti's getting desperate, teaming up with those psychopaths."

"Damn right he is," I growl. "Which is why we gotta get on top of this Hellion situation, and fast. They've got chapters all around us. If we let this go too long, we're sitting ducks."

The weight of my words hangs heavy in the air, the threat all too real for any of us to ignore.

"We're gonna need backup on this," I continue, my voice hardening with resolve. "Bring some boys in from other chapters for an extended stay to help out. We don't have enough men to keep up with all the work we have, plus the extra security we're gonna need."

As I speak, nods of agreement ripple through the room, each person realizing the gravity of the situation. I pause for a moment, allowing my words to sink in before speaking again.

"I think it's time Dom got his patch. I want to bring it to the table for a vote today. He did a damn good job helping me and X in Portland. I think we'd be a better and stronger club going forward with him as a brother."

The room falls silent, each man considering my proposal. After a few tense moments, dad speaks up, his voice cutting through the stillness.

"Alright, let's put it to a vote..."

One by one, the members voice their votes, a resounding chorus of "ayes" echoing through the room. Even the few who had their reservations in the beginning eventually give their assent, swayed by Dom's actions and my endorsement. As the final vote is cast, dad slams his hand down on the table, the sound reverberating like a judge's gavel.

"Motion carried. Let's welcome our newest brother," dad bellows, his gruff voice tinged with pride. "Patch, go get Dom."

As Patch leaves to retrieve Dom, I can't help but feel a sense of pride. Dom has proven himself time and time again, and it's only fitting that he takes his rightful place among us as a fully patched member.

The door swings open, and Patch ushers Dom inside. I can see the unease rolling off the prospect in waves as he takes in the scene before him. The entire club gathered; their gazes fixed upon him with an intensity that would shake even the most hardened of men.

"Dom," dad addresses him, his voice booming through the chapel. "Rex was just telling us how you did in Portland. Is there anything you'd like to say?"

Dom swallows hard, his Adam's apple bobbing as he gathers his composure. For a moment, he seems at a loss for words, the weight of the situation pressing down on him. Then, with a deep breath, he finds his voice.

"I know I've got a long way to go before I can truly call myself one of you. But I want you all to know that I'm in this. All the way, no matter what." He begins, his tone steady despite the nerves I know he's battling. He pauses, his gaze sweeping across the room, meeting each of our eyes in turn.

"What we did in Portland, taking down that piece of shit Ruso and dealing a blow to Moretti... that was just the beginning. I'm ready to keep fighting, to do whatever it takes to protect this club, this family."

A low rumble of approval echoes through the chapel, the brothers nodding in agreement at Dom's words.

"I know I've made mistakes in the past," Dom continues, his voice taking on a harder edge. "But those days are behind me. This club, these brothers... you're my life now. I'll never let you down."

I can see the respect in the eyes of the other members as they take in Dom's declaration. He's earned his place here, and we all know it.

Dad lets the silence linger for a few heartbeats, allowing Dom's words to sink in. Then, he rises to his feet, his imposing frame commanding the attention of every man in the room.

"Well, you heard the man," he rumbles, a hint of a smile playing at the corners of his mouth. "I think it's time we made this official. Looks like we're having a patch party."

The room erupts into cheers and raucous backslapping as the brothers surround Dom, congratulating him on earning his patch. I make my way over, pulling the kid into a bear hug.

"Proud of you," I rumble. "You earned this, fair and square."

Dom beams up at me, his eyes shining with a mix of gratitude and pride.

"Thanks, VP. I won't let you down."

I clap him on the shoulder, giving him a meaningful look.

"I know you won't, brother."

As the celebrations wind down and the chapel slowly clears out, dad motions for me to hang back. I linger behind, sensing the weight of what he wants to discuss.

"Rex, I want you to take the reins on this Hellion situation," he begins, his voice low and grave. "You and the others saw firsthand how brazen they're getting. We can't let this shit escalate any further."

I nod, my jaw clenched with determination.

"Consider it handled, Prez. I'll get the ball rolling on bringing in extra muscle from the other chapters."

"Get everyone up here that can make it for Dom's patch party. We will have it next weekend. Any member that can be spared from other chapters can stay. That will give them a week to get their shit in order."

Dad levels his steely gaze at me, his expression grave.

"I'm putting my trust in you, VP. Get this shit locked down before it blows up in our faces. We can't afford any more surprises from those psychopaths."

"You got it," I affirm, meeting his stare unflinchingly. "Consider it done."

"I'm going to go spend the evening with my granddaughter. You take a few hours to yourself, then come get her later."

"Thanks dad. Em only knows I was away working."

"I figured as much. You know that's not going to work forever. She's a smart girl."

"I know, I'll tell her everything when she is older and can understand the life. I just want to wait until she is mature enough to see the bigger picture and hope she can understand one day that sometimes the wrong thing is the right thing to do."

"That's exactly how I decided to raise you. I might be a bit biased, but I think you grew into a damn fine man. I have no doubt Em will grow into a damn fine woman." My dad walks behind me to put a reassuring hand on my shoulder. "I wouldn't worry about it son, that little girl thinks you hung the moon and the stars. You don't get love like that if you ain't doin' something right."

Dad leaves the room without another word. I sit there for a moment, then I push myself to my feet and make my way out of the chapel. First order of business is to check in with Jax and get him started on gathering intel on the Hellions' movements and operations in the area.

Next, I'll need to start reaching out to the other chapters and see who can spare some extra bodies to lend a hand. We'll need all hands-on deck for this fight.

My steps carry me towards the clubhouse basement, where I know I'll find Jax holed up in his tech cave. Sure enough, as I round the corner, I can see the glow of multiple screens illuminating his makeshift command center.

"Jax," I call out, rapping my knuckles against the doorframe. "You got a minute?"

The kid swivels around in his chair, his eyes hidden behind the glare of his monitors.

"What's up?"

I lean against the doorjamb, crossing my arms over my chest.

"Need you to start digging into the Hellions. Their movements, operations, everything you can get your hands on."

"You got it. I'll see what I can shake loose."

"Good man," I nod, already turning to leave.

"Keep me posted."

With that task delegated, it's time to find Anna. Time to stop being a pussy, get the fuck outta my head, and claim my woman.

CHAPTER 23

Anna

I'm reviewing the most recent financial documents at my desk in the office when Rex strides in with a look of determination on his face. He closes the door behind him and locks it.

“What’s wrong Rex?”

My heart pounds as he moves towards me purposefully until he's standing right in front of me. Gently, he turns my chair to face him, and I feel his right hand come around to grasp the hair at the nape of my neck, tilting my head up towards him.

His other hand comes up to gently wrap his fingers around the side of my neck while his thumb strokes my cheek tenderly.

As my eyes meet his, I see a hint of vulnerability. My heart races at his touch. The air around us thick with an unspoken desire that we both try to ignore but can't deny.

"Anna," he murmurs, his voice low and rough. "I'm done with the back-and-forth dance we've been doing. Most of that is on me, and I'm sorry for that. I've had a lot of time on my hands to think before I got out, and I'll be damned if you weren't all I could think about. I want you."

My breath caught at his words and the feeling of his hands on me. Rex confused my reaction to him with fear.

"I'm not talking about physically Anna. I get that you're not ready for that. You've been through hell, I know that. Everything else will come with time. I'm saying I want you with me. Want you with me and Em, if you'll have us."

My head bobs up and down ever so slightly as I watch the emotions flitting across his face. Rex's thumb continues its gentle, reassuring touch, never breaking eye contact with me. I can't help but lean towards him, seeking the familiar sense of security and warmth he always brings me.

"I need your words babe. I gotta know we're on the same page here. It's not just me and you in this. I can't be draggin' my daughter into this if we both aren't in it for the long haul. I won't do that to her."

"I want you too Rex. I want both of you more than anything."

Rex's lips meet mine with an intensity that leaves me breathless. His fingers tangle in my hair as one hand slides to the back of my neck, drawing me closer. I melt into his embrace, my hands gripping the front of his kutte to anchor myself.

Our kiss deepens, his tongue teasing along my lips until I part them with a soft moan. Rex takes full advantage, exploring my mouth with his own. The taste and scent of him surrounds me, intoxicating me with a desire and longing I have never felt.

I lose myself in the moment, in the feeling of Rex's solid strength pressed against me. One of his hands roams down to my waist, his touch setting my skin ablaze through the thin fabric of my top.

Rex tears his lips from mine with a ragged groan. His forehead drops to rest against mine as we both struggle to catch our breath. My fingers trace over the inked patterns on the side of his neck, feeling his rapid pulse beating beneath my fingertips.

"Anna," he rasps, his voice thick with want. “I've wanted this, wanted you, for a long time now. I was too damn afraid to make a move. I didn't want to cause more pain for you or myself. I had to figure out what I wanted. I’m sorry it took me so long.

"There are things I haven’t told you, about what happened to me. Things that might change your mind about wanting me. And I'll understand if..."

Mid-sentence, Rex straightens, and swiftly lifts me from the office chair and into his arms. He carries me effortlessly to the couch. Settling me onto his lap, my legs straddling his, he tenderly cradles my face in his warm hands.

"I do know. Those first few days at the hospital, you were in and out of consciousness. Once the doctor evaluated you, treated your wounds, and understood the full extent of your injuries, they discussed everything with Sarah. I was with her for that conversation.

I'm sorry if you didn’t want me to know. I may not know all the details, but I know what those sick fucks did to you. Violated you in the worst way possible. How could you ever think I wouldn’t want you because of that?"

He knows... he knows the depths of my suffering, the worst of what was done to me. A wave of shame washes over me, hot tears stinging my eyes.

Rex must see the turmoil on my face and pulls me tighter against him, cradling me in his strong embrace.

"Anna, baby, look at me," he murmurs, tilting my chin up. "None of that was your fault, you hear me? Those motherfuckers who hurt you are the ones who should be ashamed, not you. It wasn’t your choice, Anna; they took that from you."

I search his eyes, finding nothing but fierce protectiveness and tenderness reflecting back at me. Slowly, I nod, letting the truth of his words start to sink in. He doesn't see me as ruined or damaged goods. In his eyes, I'm still worthy of being loved and cared for.

I lean into the solid strength of his chest, letting the steady thump of his heartbeat soothe me. Rex's arms tighten around me as he presses a lingering kiss to the top of my head.

The shadows of my past no longer loom so large when I'm surrounded by his unwavering devotion chasing away the darkness. Here in his arms is where I belong.

My fingers trace over the stubbled line of his jaw as I drink in his features. The intense blue of his eyes, the sharp angles of his face softened by the emotion playing across it.

"After everything... I never thought I'd be able to be close with anyone like this. To feel this way. I don't know what I did to deserve you, Rex, but I'm so damn thankful for it."

"Way I see it, we both got a second chance neither of us expected. I'd be a damn fool to let you slip away." He brushes a loose curl away from my face. "You in this with me?"

"I'm with you."

His eyes burn with an intensity that sends a shiver down my spine.

"You're everything to me, Anna. You and my little girl... you're my world now."

As Rex's lips meet mine again, I give in to the moment and allow his hands to explore my body. I press myself against him.

His rough fingers trail down my spine, sending shivers up my back as they reach the hem of my shirt. His fingers trace the curve of my waist, dipping into the waistband of my jeans. My body arches towards him as he pulls me closer. I moan softly as our bodies grind against each other. His lips find their way to my neck, teasing every nerve ending with his skilled mouth.

Rex trails kisses along my jaw line, leaving a trail of fire in their wake. His hands continue their descent, resting on my hips before sliding around my backside until his big hands are caressing and squeezing my ass. The way he touches me is intimate and tender, something I've never experienced before.

I feel desired and cherished, valued in a way that is completely new to me.

He reaches the sensitive spot just below my ear, nibbling gently on it before whispering, "You're so fucking beautiful, Anna."

I close my eyes and lean into his touch, feeling more alive than I have in years. His hands continue their exploration, tracing the curve of my hips and sliding under the waistband of my pants to rest on the soft skin of my lower back. My body responds to his touch with a heat that I can't control.

"Rex," I breathe his name on a soft exhale. I don't know what will happen next, but I know I don't want him to stop.

He pulls back slightly to look into my eyes, his gaze filled with desire and tenderness.

"I want you so much," he murmurs before capturing my lips once more in a deep kiss that leaves me breathless and wanting more.

My nails lightly rake over the hard planes of his back as I pull him flush against me. I crave his touch, his closeness, after so long feeling alone.

His hands grip my hips firmly as he grinds against me, letting me feel how much he wants me. I gasp at the delicious friction, arching into him wantonly.

Suddenly he stills, pulling back slightly. Rex's eyes are clouded with a mixture of desire and... guilt?

"We have to stop," he murmurs regretfully. "Not like this."

I blink up at him in confusion, my brain struggling to process his words over the haze of arousal.

"W-what? Why?"

Rex lets out a breath, bringing his hand up to tenderly stroke my cheek.

"You deserve so much more than me taking you on this damn couch like some back-alley whore."

My eyes widen at his words. Instantly feeling self-conscious and small under his intense gaze. I jerk back from him and his words. Rex seems to realize how that came out and quickly tries to backtrack.

"Shit, Anna, that's not what I meant." He drops his forehead to rest against mine. "You're everything to me, which is why I want to do this right."

I blink rapidly, trying to process Rex's words as a torrent of emotions crashes over me. Anger, shame, frustration. They all swirl together in a confusing maelstrom. Suddenly I'm filled with anger and I'm not really sure why.

"You were doing it right Rex!" I yell at him, even though I don't think my anger is aimed at him.

"You were letting it be my choice."

My voice cracks with anguish as the next words tumble out.

"I've never had a choice. I've never had sex before because I wanted to. It was never a choice I was able to make."

Rex's arms tighten around me, pulling me against his chest as my body trembles with the force of my emotions. He strokes my hair soothingly, murmuring softly.

"You're in control now. You always have a choice with me. Always."

"I'm sorry. I didn't mean to freak out like that."

"Don't apologize," he rumbles. "That's exactly why I want to do this right. You will never feel the touch of another hand that takes from you again. The only touch you'll ever know, ever feel, the rest of your life will be mine. I promise you baby, when I give it to you, I'll make damn sure it's so damn good, I'm the only one you'll ever remember."

CHAPTER 24

Rex

I stand on the patio behind the club house while my dad gives a speech, kicking off Dom's patch party. I survey the scene before me with a sense of pride. The compound is absolutely packed, brothers from all ten Rebel Sons chapters having made the journey for Dom's patching ceremony. This is what the club is truly about.

Some of these guys have ridden four or five days straight to be here, leaving their homes and families behind without hesitation. They make that sacrifice every single time, honoring the commitment and showing up for their brothers. It's the loyalty and respect that binds us all together.

My dad motions for Dom to step forward.

"Dominic Sullivan, come up here, son."

Dom strides up to the makeshift stage, you can tell the kid is a mix of nerves and excitement. This is the moment he's been working towards for over a year. I give him a clap on the back as he passes by me.

Our President's hand tightly grasps Dom's prospect kutte.

"This kutte you've been wearing represented your commitment to our way of life. You've made sacrifices, shed blood, sweat, and tears to earn your place in our brotherhood."

There's a heavy pause as my dad lets those words sink in. Every brother here knows exactly what that kutte means.

"But today, you shed that prospect skin." With one forceful tug, dad rips the kutte from Dom's back.

A raucous cheer erupts from the crowd as Beau reaches for the crisp new kutte draped over his arm. This one bears the full Rebel Sons colors, marking Dom as one of us.

"The bond between us is unbreakable, tempered by the battles we've fought side-by-side, the blood we've shed for each other. We're more than just a club; together we're a force of fucking nature, but above all we're family."

As one, the group of bikers surrounding me chant the oath of the Rebel Sons. "We ride together, we rise together, we die together. Forever Sons." This is what it truly means to be a Son.

My dad presents Dom with his new kutte, the leather pristine and unmarked, save for the meticulously stitched patches.

"Dom, welcome to the family brother. We're honored to have you."

The crowd erupts in cheers and applause as Dom proudly slips into his new kutte. I can't help but grin, remembering that same feeling of acceptance and belonging when I was patched in almost 15 years ago.

I catch Dom's eye and give him a subtle nod of respect. He's more than earned this. Paying his dues to get here.

I raise my beer in salute as my father's words ring out across the compound.

"Tonight, we not only celebrate Dom, but we also celebrate the fall of the Moretti empire. Each of our ten chapters came together to dismantle the largest trafficking ring in the entire country. That's an accomplishment to be damn proud of."

A deafening roar of cheer erupts from the crowd, proudly displaying the Rebel Sons colors on their kuttes.

"We might be on the wrong side of the law more than the right," dad continues, "but we are still damn good people at the end of the day."

I take a long pull from my beer as my eyes scan the familiar faces all around. These are my brothers, my family. We've bled together, fought together, lived by a code that transcends societal rules and norms. Yeah, we're an outlaw club. But we live by a strict moral code. Loyalty, respect, and protecting those who can't protect themselves.

My gaze lands on Anna where she stands amongst the crowd, her beauty shining bright even in this rough environment. She's living proof of what we fight against, a survivor of the depravity we've worked to dismantle.

Seeing her surrounded by my brothers, I know she's finally found the security and safety she deserves. We may be rough around the edges, but she's family now. We protect our own with everything we've got.

My dad finishes his speech, his gravelly voice echoing out into the crowd with authority.

"Tonight, we revel in our victories. Let loose, have a hell of a good time. Come tomorrow, we go to war.

Cheers of approval rises up from the crowd of leather-clad bikers. The cheer is guttural, primal, like a pack of wolves baying for blood. We may have crippled Moretti and his syndicate, but this fight is far from over. Those pricks were just the beginning. The Hellions want a war? They've got one.

These men would follow me straight into the pits of hell itself without hesitation. That's the strength of our bond. I raise my beer high.

"To the Rebel Sons! Death before dishonor, brothers!"

* * *

I scan the crowd, my eyes landing on Anna amongst a group of old ladies from the other chapters. She's laughing with Cassandra at something Sarah said. Even in the dim lighting she's fucking beautiful.

As I start making my way over, I get stopped by Wolf from the Trinidad chapter. He's deep in conversation with Jett, our club secretary.

"I heard you're sticking around for a while brother. I was surprised to hear it." I say, clasping hands with Wolf, we pull each other into a back slapping hug.

"Your old man asked for all hands-on deck. You know I got too much respect for Beau to say no," Wolf replies gruffly.

I raise an eyebrow. "You sure your chapter's okay with their Prez being gone?"

Wolf shrugs, "my VP is solid, the boys got it covered. Like I said, when your dad asks for help, I'm there."

Giving him an appreciative slap on the back, "good to have you here, man. I got some things to take care of, but I'll catch you later."

Finally reaching Anna, I lean in close so only she can hear me over the music and laughter. "You wanna get outta here for a bit? Just you and me?"

"Yeah, I do."

I offer her my hand, pulling her to her feet and leading her away from the crowd.

I lead Anna behind the townhouses towards the tree line at the back of the property. There's a small clearing with a trail that winds through the trees, one she didn't seem to know about.

"Where does this lead?" she asks, hesitating for a moment.

"There's a little pond back here," I explain. "Thought we could use some privacy for a bit."

I pull a flashlight from my back pocket and click it on, illuminating the narrow dirt path ahead of us. Anna falls into step beside me as we venture into the trees.

"My grandpa found this place when they were first setting up the compound years ago," I tell her. "He built a tiny one-room cabin right on the edge of the pond."

Memories come flooding back as we follow the familiar trail. Times when I was just a kid, coming out here with Gunnar to get away and just be kids for a while. We'd spend entire summers swimming in that pond.

"Gunnar and I used to come out here all the time when we were younger," I continue. "Since we were both raised in the club, it was one of the only places we could truly get away, you know?"

The trail opens up to a small clearing, the moonlight glinting off the still waters of the pond. The old cabin is barely visible through the trees, its weathered wood blending into the scenery. I stop and turn to face Anna, her eyes wide with wonder.

"It's beautiful up here," her voice barely above a whisper as she takes in our secluded surroundings. "So quiet. You can barely hear the music from the clubhouse. That pond is the size of a lake."

"Yeah, that's what Gunnar and I always liked about it." I guide her towards the old cabin, the front porch extending out over the still waters of the pond like a dock. Pushing open the weathered door, I motion for her to go inside first.

The place is still the same as when I was a kid. A small table shoved against one wall, a cooler filled with beers that I stashed here earlier, and a rickety old bed crammed into the far corner. A couple of well-used fishing poles lean against the wall, remnants of lazy summer days spent out here.

"You want a beer?" I ask, already reaching into the cooler and popping the caps off two bottles.

"Sure," Anna replies, taking the cold beer from my outstretched hand.

I pause for a moment, the bottle nearly at my lips, as I watch her take a pull from the amber bottle. My gaze lingers on the gentle curve of her lips wrapped around the bottle's opening.

"You ever been night fishing before?" I ask, gesturing towards the rickety old poles propped up against the wall.

Anna's head shakes, a playful grin just starting to show at the corners of her mouth.

"It's pitch black out there. How are we supposed to see what we're doing?"

"That's the best time to go for catfish. They're more active at night, easier to catch when they're feeding. Gunnar and I used to stay up all night, drinking beer we'd steal from our dads and trying to out-fish each other." Turning back towards Anna, I raise an expectant eyebrow. "So? You wanna give it a shot?"

There is a flicker of amusement on her face as she pauses to think about my suggestion.

"No, I don't think so. But maybe you could bring me out here again sometime to try."

I place the pole back against the wall. I hear the soft clink of Anna's bottle as she sets her beer down on the old table behind me. Turning back around, she's right in front of me, her gaze intense like I've never seen before. She takes the beer bottle from my grasp and sets it down next to hers. Then, she's all over me, her hands wrapping around the back of my neck and pulling me towards her as she presses her lips against mine.

For a split second, I'm taken aback by her bold move. But then, my instincts kick in and I kiss her back. My arms wrapping around her waist, drawing her body closer to mine.

Anna's grip on the hair at the back of my neck tightens, her lips pressed hard against mine. The tang of beer lingers on her lips, igniting a hunger within me. My hands roam down to grasp her hips. I grind her against my growing erection that's aching for release against the confines of my jeans.

A deep, primal growl from the depths of my chest rises up as I feel her nails rake over the sensitive skin on the back of my neck. My lips capture her full bottom lip, teasing it between my teeth and giving it a light nip before soothing it with my tongue. The pretty little whimpers that fall from her parted lips almost make me fucking groan with need.

Spinning us around, I walk Anna backwards until her legs hit the edge of the old bed. With a smirk and a gentle shove, I push Anna down onto the creaky mattress. She looks up at me with those beautiful dark, longing eyes as she props herself up on her elbows. Her chest rises and falls with each breath she takes.

I don't give her a chance to catch her breath before I'm on her again. Lowering myself onto her, I can feel the heat radiating from Anna's body, her eyes burning with desire.

"Come here," she whispers, pulling me down to her waiting lips. Our mouths meet in a frenzy, her hands grasping at my hair and urging me closer. "I've been wanting this for so long."

With one hand braced beside her head, I let the other roam down the curves of her body. My fingertips glide over the silky-smooth skin of her thigh before sliding up beneath the hem of her skirt. A quiet gasp escapes her when I reach the velvety, slick heat of her pussy. I growl into her open mouth, a sound born from desire and surprise, when I discover she's not wearing anything underneath.

“Aren’t you just full of fuckin’ surprises tonight.”

Anna arches her hips, silently asking me for more, and I am more than willing to comply. My hand moves further down, resting on her throbbing core. I can feel the wetness of her arousal on my fingers. She lets out a soft moan when I tease her entrance with two fingers. I hold back, denying her what I know she truly wants.

I plant a trail of hot, open-mouthed kisses along her delicate neck and jawline before reaching the tempting curves of her breasts. With skillful movements, I pull her shirt up and over her head, revealing them gorgeous tits to my hungry gaze.

"Fuck, you're beautiful," I rasp, taking a moment to simply admire the sight of her laid out before me.

My mouth damn near waters as I dip my head and capture one rosy nipple between my lips. Anna's back arches as I swirl my tongue around her hardened nipple before giving it a light nip with my teeth. She cries out, her fingers fisting tightly in my hair to hold me in place.

Switching my attention to her other breast, I let my free hand drift down between her thighs once more. This time I don't tease, sinking two fingers knuckle-deep inside her sweet heat. Anna lets out a long moan as I set a steady rhythm, my thumb circling her sensitive clit.

"Rex... oh god..."

The sounds of her ragged gasps and the way her body is trembling beneath me has my cock aching, straining painfully against my jeans. I crave to be inside her, to feel her gripping my cock. But not before I make her come on my fingers. Not before she's a quivering mess beneath me.

Without warning, I plunge three fingers inside her wet heat, curling them to rub her g-spot. I watch as her eyes roll back into her head, and she cries out my name like it's the sweetest fuckin' thing she's ever tasted.

"That's it... come for me Anna," I growl in her ear, picking up the pace of my thrusts. "Come for me, baby." Anna's nails dig into my shoulder blades as she arches her hips off the bed, meeting each of my thrusts. Her pussy clenches tightly, spasming around my fingers.

Anna's body tenses, her head flung back, body arching off the bed as she comes hard. Her face contorts in pleasure, her mouth open in a silent scream as her eyes squeeze shut. Her tits bounce with each thrust of my hand between her thighs.

Lifting my head from her breasts, I lock eyes with her.

"You good, gorgeous?"

Anna smiles, running her fingers through my hair.

"More than good."

"You want more?" I ask, needing to hear her say it. I don't want to be another man who takes from her.

"Hell yeah," she exclaims, the words slipping out before she even realizes what she's said.

I couldn't hold back the laugh that burst out of me. "Full of fuckin' surprises."

Withdrawing my fingers, I get to my feet beside the bed. I take a condom out of my back pocket and toss it on the bed. Then make quick work of unbuckling my belt and shoving my jeans down, freeing my throbbing length. Anna's eyes widen momentarily when she sees my full size.

I position myself between her parted thighs, allowing the broad head of my cock to slowly tease her slick entrance. Anna's body writhes beneath me, her back arching as she gasps for more, trying to take me deeper. But I resist, wanting to draw out the moment that I've been waiting for.

"You want this, baby?" I rasp, my voice already wrecked with desire. "Tell me how bad you need it."

"Yes, Rex... please, I need you inside me," she whimpers, her nails raking down my chest and stomach.

I grab the condom, tearing it open with my teeth and sliding it down my shaft. I lean down over Anna, so we are face to face.

"Eyes on me Anna. I need you to hear me." I speak gruffly against her parted lips. "You need to be sure, cause as soon as I get a real taste of that hellfire inside you... ain't no chance of me turnin' back. You'll be mine."

"I think I've been yours since you carried me out of that basement."

Without hesitation, I'm burying myself deep inside Anna with one powerful thrust. Anna's eyes squeeze shut, and her mouth forms a perfect 'O' of ecstasy as her pussy stretches deliciously around my thick cock.

In that instant, I'm paralyzed, overtaken by the sensation of her tight, hot cunt pulsing around me. She moves her hips in a slow, circular motion, urging me to move, trying to take me even deeper.

Bracing myself on my elbows, I cradle Anna's head in my hands. I press my lips to hers, taking in the sweet taste of her lips and breathing in her soft moans that fill the air as I start to move.

I set a punishing pace, each thrust driving into her again and again until the only sounds are the creaking of the old bedsprings beneath us, and the raw, primal, obscene slaps of our bodies colliding together.

Anna gives as good as she gets, meeting me thrust for thrust. Her nails scoring lines down my back as she clings to me desperately. I can feel her inner muscles starting to clench around my cock, her whole-body tensing as she nears the edge.

"That's it, baby... let go for me," I growl against the slick column of her throat. "I want to feel you coming on my cock."

Anna's piercing cries of ecstasy echo throughout the small cabin as she falls apart. I don't let up, pounding into her through the waves of her climax until her body is shaking, overstimulated with pleasure. Only when the inner walls of her delicious pussy stop milking my dick do I finally still my hips, coming harder than I ever have as I drive myself deep inside her one last time.

Bracing my weight on one arm, I guide Anna's face towards mine with the gentle touch of my free hand. Her eyes are heavy with satisfaction, her lips slightly parted as she catches her breath. I drink in the sight of her like a man dying of thirst. I lower myself for one last kiss from her full lips.

When I finally pull away, I can't quite read the expression on Anna's face.

“What’s wrong baby? Did I hurt you?” Dread fills me and my gut sinks as I see tears forming in her eyes. “I’m so sorry.”

“No, Rex.” She’s shaking her head as she puts a hand on my cheek. “You didn’t hurt me. You kept your promise. Your touch is the only one I feel now.”

"I'll never make you a promise I can't keep."

I knew in that moment that I would burn down the whole goddamn world for this woman.

CHAPTER 25

Anna

I'm lying across Rex's chest, my head rising and falling with each of his steady breaths. I feel happier than I have in a long time, maybe ever.

"You're really okay with everything?" Rex asks, his voice a low rumble against my ear. There's a hint of concern laced into the words. "That was a little more aggressive than I thought our first time would go."

I tilt my head up to meet his intense gaze, offering a reassuring smile. "I'm better than okay. " My fingers trace the ridges of the scars crisscrossing his chest as I drink in the reality of this moment with him.

A deafening boom rips through the air, shaking the very foundations of the cabin. I jolt upright, Rex's arms instinctively tightening around me as the windows rattle violently. My heart pounds, the phantom echoes of gunfire and explosions flooding my mind.

"Hey, you're okay," Rex soothes, sensing my panic. He places a tender kiss on my forehead before reluctantly pulling away. "But we need to get dressed. Now."

In one fluid motion, he swings his powerful frame off the bed and begins hastily tugging on his clothes. I force myself to follow his lead, trying to tamp down the rising fear as I slip into my jean skirt and tank top with shaking hands.

Rex retrieves his gun from the nightstand and racks the slide, the metallic click sending a chill down my spine.

"Take this. Keep your finger off the trigger unless you're ready to use it." His voice is gruff but tender.

I take the gun from Rex's outstretched hand, my fingers trembling slightly as I wrap them around the grip.

"Rex, what's happening?" I ask, my voice laced with fear and uncertainty.

He gives me a reassuring squeeze on my shoulder.

"I don't know, but I'm going to find out. Stay here, no one will come out here. It's the safest place for you until I know what the fuck is going on. Lock the door behind me, and don't open it for anyone except me. Understand?"

I nod, my heart pounding in my chest and the sound of the explosion still ringing in my ears. Rex leaves and I lock the door as instructed, clutching the gun tightly in my hands.

The cabin falls silent, save for the sound of my own shaky breaths. I move to the window, peeking out cautiously, but I can't see anything except the trees swaying in the wind. Anxiety coils in the pit of my stomach as I wait, praying for Rex to return unharmed.

I don't know how much time has passed, but the silence is deafening. Ten minutes? Fifteen? Every second that ticks by amplifies the worry gnawing at my insides. Worst-case scenarios start flashing through my mind, each one more terrifying than the last.

Then I think about Emmalynn. What if she's scared out of her mind right now? She was staying at Sarah and Jake's place for Dom's patch party, with Marlene watching over her and baby Barrett. A knot forms in my throat at the thought of that sweet little girl in danger. And Marlene... she's in her late 70s. She wouldn't be able to defend herself if something truly terrible was unfolding.

My grip tightens on the gun in my hands. I can't just sit here, not knowing if Em and the others are safe. Rex made me promise to stay put, but he doesn't understand... I have to get to them.

Steeling my nerves, I inch towards the door and press my ear against it, straining to hear any signs of movement outside. When I'm met with stillness, I slowly unlock it and crack it open just a sliver, peering out cautiously. The coast seems clear for now. I slip out of the cabin, my heart pounding as I dart between the trees, constantly scanning my surroundings for any potential threats...

I clutch the gun tightly as I approach the tree line at the back of the townhouses. The screams, gunfire, and small explosions grow louder, making my heart race. Something is terribly wrong. I walk slowly and cautiously, trying not to make a sound.

As I reach the point where the trees open up to the backyard of the townhouses, I stop and scan the area from their cover. I don't see any movement.

Mustering my courage, I run as fast as I can to the back door of Sarah's house. They rarely lock the doors on the compound, but I know there's a spare key under a flowerpot by the door. My hands tremble as I retrieve the key and unlock the door. I quickly slip inside, locking it behind me. The house is eerily quiet compared to the chaos outside. I pause for a moment, listening intently for any signs of life, but there's nothing.

I move slowly through the house, my heart pounding in my chest. First, I head to Barrett's nursery, pushing open the door as quietly as I can. The room is empty. A sick feeling settles in my stomach as I turn and make my way upstairs.

At the top of the stairs, I see the door to the spare room is slightly ajar. This must be where Em is staying. I take a deep, steadying breath and push the door open, the gun gripped tightly in my trembling hands.

The sight before me makes me freeze. Marlene is sitting at the foot of the bed, one arm cradling Barrett protectively against her chest. In her other hand, she's clutching a shotgun pointed directly at me.

Relief washes over me as I realize they're all safe, but it's quickly tempered by Marlene's fierce expression. Her eyes are hard and determined, every muscle in her body tense. I raise my hands slowly in surrender, the gun dangling from my fingers.

"Marlene, it's me, Anna," I whisper, not wanting to wake

Emmalynn who is sleeping soundly behind her.

Marlene's steely gaze doesn't waver. "I know who you are, girl," she says gruffly. "Now tell me what in the hell is goin' on out there before I blow your head clean off."

I raise my hands in a placating gesture, trying to convey that I mean no harm.

"Marlene, I have no idea what's going on out there," I explain, my voice barely above a whisper. "Rex and I were at the pond behind the houses when we heard an explosion. It shook the whole cabin."

Marlene's brow furrows, but she keeps the shotgun trained on me, her grip unwavering. I swallow hard, suddenly very aware of the weight of the gun in my own hand.

"Rex left to find out what was happening," I continue quickly. "He told me to stay put, that I'd be safe in the cabin. I did for a while, and then..." My voice catches in my throat as I glance over at Emmalynn's sleeping form. "I got worried about the kids. I knew you were alone with them, so I came here."

Marlene studies me intently for a moment, her eyes searching mine. Finally, after what feels like an eternity, she slowly lowers the shotgun, letting out a weary sigh.

"You did the right thing, comin' to check on us," she says, her tone softening slightly. "But you shouldn't have come alone, not with whatever the hell is goin' on out there."

I nod, relief flooding through me as the tension in the room dissipates. "I know, I just... I had to make sure Em and Barrett were okay."

Marlene gives me a small, understanding smile, and in that moment, I see the wisdom and strength that has allowed her to survive so much over the years.

"Look out the window that overlooks the compound and see what's happening. Stay low to the ground." Marlene orders.

I slowly crawl towards the window, keeping low to avoid being spotted from outside. My heart pounds in my chest as I peek over the ledge, trying to make sense of the chaos unfolding before my eyes.

"The gate..." I whisper, my voice trembling. "It's gone." The large gate at the entrance to the compound is nothing more than a twisted heap of smoldering metal, flames licking at the debris.

Marlene's face grows grave as she takes in my words. I force myself to continue surveying the scene, swallowing hard.

"There's a car on fire right by the gate too." My gaze shifts to the compound itself, and I have to stifle a gasp. Men are fighting everywhere, fists and chains swinging wildly.

"There are men everywhere." My grip tightens on the gun in my hands. "Marlene, the other guys are wearing kuttes too, a red devil's face patch."

"The Hellions," she says grimly.

I give a small nod, my eyes widening as I spot a familiar figure moving purposefully across the compound. Beau is making his way towards the house, despite the chaos surrounding him. Relief washes over me at the sight of him.

"Beau," I breathe. "He's heading this way."

Marlene rises to her feet, adjusting her grip on the shotgun.

"Go let him in, girl. But be quick about it and keep your head down."

I scramble to my feet and hurry downstairs, my heart hammering against my ribs. Steeling my nerves, I crack open the front door just enough to peer out cautiously. That's when I see Beau in a heated argument with someone. They're standing close, both wielding guns pointed directly at each other.

Beau shifts his stance slightly, and that's when I see who he's arguing with... my father. A chill runs down my spine as I take in his cold, unforgiving glare locked onto Beau.

After everything the club has done for me, I can't let my father hurt Beau. He's been more of a father to me than Tony ever was. Steeling my nerves, I slowly creep out of the house, keeping low to avoid drawing any attention. As I get closer, a twig snaps loudly beneath my foot.

Beau's head whips in my direction at the sound. In that split second of distraction, Tony seizes the opportunity. Time seems to slow as I watch the barrel of his gun rise and the muzzle flash.

A scream rips from my throat as Beau crumples to the ground. Without a second thought, I raise the gun in my shaking hands and pull the trigger again and again, unloading the entire clip at my father.

My father crumples to the ground, blood seeping from the bullet holes in his chest. I don't feel the rush of satisfaction I thought I would at finally being free of his evil grip on my life. There's only a hollow emptiness.

Shoving those feelings aside, I rush over to Beau. He's lying motionless on the ground, a gunshot wound to the head painting the grass crimson beneath him. I press my shaking hands over the injury, desperately trying to stem the flow of blood.

"Beau, stay with me," I plead, my voice cracking with panic. "Everything's going to be okay, you're going to be okay."

A deep chuckle comes from behind me, sending a chill down my spine. "Don't lie to the man. He's as good as dead. Just like every other Rebel Son on this compound tonight."

I slowly turn to face the source of the gravelly voice. A massive man with a shaved head and numerous scars glares down at me through narrowed eyes. The Hellions' red devil's face patch on his kutte leaves no doubt as to his allegiance.

He raises his gun, the barrel pointing squarely at my head. "Oh yeah, you're dead too, sweetheart."

My breath catches in my throat as I watch his finger start to tighten on the trigger. This is it. I close my eyes, bracing for the inevitable...

CHAPTER 26

Rex

Amidst the mayhem surrounding me, a chilling scream pierces through the air, causing my heart to damn near stop beating. The sound of nine gunshots echo through the night, one right after the other, each one hitting me like a physical blow.

I break into a full sprint towards the townhouses, following the direction of Anna's scream. It's the same route my father took to check on Gram and the kids. As I turn the corner, everything seems to move in slow motion.

Anna is crouched over my father's motionless body, using herself as a human shield. His eyes stare blankly ahead, lifeless, with a bullet wound on the side of his head. A second body lies nearby in a crumpled heap. Anna's head is turned away from me, facing Hatchet, the president of the Hell's Hellions. He towers over her, his gun aimed directly at her head.

I hear the sound of a gunshot before I can even raise my own gun. Everything around me comes to a standstill. I can't bear to go through this again. To have someone I love taken from me right in front of my eyes. There's no way I'll make it through that pain again.

My mind is struggling to keep up with the scene unfolding before me. I watch as Hatchet's lifeless body falls to the ground. And there behind him stands Maverick, his arm extended with a gun in hand.

“Anna!” I run to her, taking her into my arms and pulling her close. “You need to get inside the house now.” She looks up at me with a tear-stained face, filled with terror and desperation.

"Beau’s still alive," she chokes out. "We have to get him to a hospital, we have to help him, Rex."

I turn my eyes to Maverick and see the shock and disbelief written all over his face. This is his first-time laying eyes on his old man, and he’s lying half dead on the ground with a bullet through his skull.

"Maverick! Get your ass moving, we don’t have time for this shit!” I shout at him, trying to break through whatever daze he’s in.

“Help me get dad inside." Together we lift our father's lifeless body. Each step feels like I'm wading through quicksand as we carry him into Jake’s house, Anna in front, leading the way.

“Baby, get a towel to hold pressure on dad’s wound.” She rushes off as Maverick and I lay our father down on the couch, his head lolling to the side. I grip my dad’s hand tightly, “You’re gonna be okay old man. I’m gonna go kill all these motherfuckers and then we’ll get you outta here.” I keep my voice steady, masking the turmoil raging inside me.

Dad groans in pain, squeezing my hand back slightly. Tears that I will not allow to fall, sting the backs of my eyes at the little sign of life from my dad.

Anna rushes back with a clean towel. Her hands shaking as she presses it firmly against the bloody hole in dad's head.

"I'm so sorry. God, Beau, I'm so sorry." Anna mutters under hear breath. I hold her tightly trying to get her to calm down.

"He's going to be okay, right?" She asks, her face filled with anguish and tears falling from her beautiful brown eyes.

"He's going to be fine, sweetheart. I need you to stay with him until I get back."

"Please don't leave." Anna's eyes are wide with terror. The fear in her voice cuts straight to my core.

I cup Anna's face in my hands, "I have to go. With dad down, the responsibility of leading these men falls on me. Those are my brothers, my family out there fighting. I will stand next to them and fight until every last one of those Hellion fucks are dead." I wipe away the tears flowing down her cheeks with the pads of my thumbs.

"Don't worry about me. I'll always come back." I promised, knowing damn well that might not be true. I touch my forehead to Anna's, "I love you."

"I love you too. You told me you'd never make me a promise you can't keep." Anna whispers.

"I know I did, and I have every fucking intention on keeping this one." I turn away quickly and head for the door.

“Let's go brother,” I motion for Maverick to follow, as he falls in step behind me. My mind is a tornado of rage and anguish as we exit the townhouse.

Stepping out of the door, the scene unfolding in front of us is one of pure fucking chaos. Brothers engage in brutal hand-to-hand combat, while the deafening sound of gunfire echoes around us. Maverick and I move quickly to join the fight. We move seamlessly together, like a well-oiled machine. One by one, we eliminate one Hellion after another.

They caught us by surprise, but these bastards made a grave mistake. With all ten chapters of the Rebel Sons gathered at the compound, they stand no chance against our overwhelming numbers. Each of my brothers fighting fiercely for one another, driven by loyalty.

I watch Maverick, a man I barely know, but my brother none the less, cut through the enemy with the same merciless precision as my most trusted brothers. We move in perfect sync like we've been doing this together all our lives. Protecting each other's backs as we push forward into the chaos.

“You traitorous rat bastard!” The vicious snarl leaves the Hellion’s lips as he lunges at Maverick. A look of pure hatred in his eyes and a machete gripped tightly in his right hand. Before Maverick has time to turn around, I fire a single shot that pierces through the prick’s skull, dead center between his eyes.

In a spray of blood and brain matter, he falls to the ground. The machete inches away from slashing Maverick's throat.

A frenzied looking Hellion charges at me desperately, from my side. I sidestep his clumsy attack and drive my knee up into his stomach, knocking the wind out of him. As he doubles over, I bring the butt of my gun down on the back of his neck, dropping him to the ground.

Another Hellion is on me in an instant, this one brandishing a wicked-looking knife. I quickly catch his wrist mid-strike, twisting it viciously with all my force until I hear the unmistakable snap of bone. The bastard screams in pain as the knife falls to the ground. My fist connects with his nose in a spray of crimson. He collapses onto the ground beside the Hellion I killed before him.

One by one, I watch as Hellions are being picked off with precision, each brought down by a single shot. I quickly search the rooftops for the sharpshooter. I spot Jake on top the clubhouse roof. His rifle steady, his aim focused on the enemy with calculated accuracy.

He was a trained sniper during his time in the Marines, and now those skills are being put to good use as he takes down one Hellion after another in a calculated strike. I watch as he eliminates at least 15 targets in rapid succession, each shot hitting its intended target with deadly precision.

From his vantage point on top the roof, Jake's stream of gunfire wreaks havoc on the Hellions. Confusion and chaos sparking within their ranks. Their men falling one by one as Jake's rifle barks out a cadence of death. Hellion forces are falling quickly, creating an opening for my men to advance forward.

Maverick and I push forward, stepping over the dead bodies. A pained groan catches my attention, causing my head to turn in its direction. My brother from the Reno chapter, Crow, is being taken down under a hail of gunfire. Mav and I drop the two Hellions responsible, and I quickly assess Crow's injuries.

"Hang in there, Crow," I try to slow the bleeding, but there are too many bullet holes in my brother's body. I can't keep up with them all. Patch is a few yards away. My voice cuts through the fading sounds of gunfire as I yell for his help.

"Patch! Get the fuck over here!" Patch deftly dodges incoming rounds as he sprints towards us. He drops to his knees beside Crow's still form, eyes scanning to evaluate the numerous bullet wounds riddling his body. Our eyes meet, and Patch gravely shakes his head, there is no saving our brother.

"Patch, you need to get to Jake's house now. Beau was shot in the head, but he's still alive. Anna is with him." Patch's eyes go wide with alarm at the news of my father's dire condition. Before he can respond, I turn to Maverick. "Go with Patch. Cover him and help with whatever he needs." Maverick nods curtly, his expression one of steely resolve as he falls in beside Patch.

“Whatever he needs, let’s go Patch.” Maverick starts to move.

For a brief moment, confusion flickers across Patch's face.

"Who the fuck is he?"

"I'll explain later, for now, he's one of us," I hiss. "Now get moving, both of you. I'll be right behind you."

Crouched low, behind a pickup truck, Jett and Talon run to my side, flanking me, as Patch and Maverick take off towards the houses.

"What the fuck happened?" I demand, my voice edged with a mixture of fury and dread.

Talon's jaw tightens as he relays the grim details.

"They blew the gate. Parker and a prospect from Hazard were on guard. They didn't stand a chance, died in the blast."

A knot forms in the pit of my stomach at the loss of two more brothers. But Talon isn't finished.

"Dom's girlfriend was at the gate, waiting to be let in. It was her car that was engulfed. She didn't make it."

"God dammit!" I explode in a rage, slamming my fist against the truck.

Jett's voice breaks through the tense silence. "Looks like there's maybe ten Hellions left," he reports, a hint of relief in his tone. "The dumb fucks finally figured out they're outnumbered and started retreating."

"We have to get to the van. Can’t waste any more time on these bastards." I bark. "We need to kill the rest of these motherfuckers and quick. Prez is in bad shape and we gotta get him to the hospital." My throat tightens, the words like swallowing shards of glass. "He took a bullet to the head."

My eyes quickly scan the rooftop, desperately searching for any sign of Jake. "Jake!" I yell, my voice rising above the fading sounds of gunfire. "Mow the rest of these motherfuckers down! We can't waste any more time on this bullshit!"

Talon turns to me, "I'll go grab the van."

"Find Gunnar and Wolf on your way, tell them to get a group ready to escort us to the hospital and get over to Jake's ready to move." Every second feels like an hour with my father's life hanging in the balance.

As Jett and I make our way to Jake's house. We burst through the door to find Patch working to stabilize my dad, while Anna maintains steady pressure on the gunshot wound to his head.

"It's time to get the fuck outta here, Patch. You ready to move him?"

Patch meets my gaze, his expression grim but determined. "Yeah VP, we're good to go."

With Maverick and Jett's help, we carefully lift my father's limp form and rush him outside to the waiting van. Before climbing in, I turn to Talon.

"Tell Jake to take the reins while I'm gone. He needs to get in contact with all the other chapter presidents, do a headcount. Secure the perimeter, then sweep every inch of this compound to make sure none of those pricks are hiding anywhere. I want two brothers guarding every entrance to Jake's house."

I climb into the back of the van; I take my father's hand in mine as Patch continues working to stabilize him. Just as we're passing through the smoldering remains of the compound's gate, Patch's voice cuts through the tension in the van.

"Fuck! He's fading!" Patch curses, immediately starting CPR on my dad. After a few moments he checks again. "No heartbeat."

My heart sinks in my stomach as I helplessly watch another person I love die in front of me, and there isn't a damn thing I can do to stop it.

EPILOGUE

Anna

I sit across from Gunnar at the large oak desk in my office, poring over the club's financial records.

"Okay, so we've got the insurance payments from the Hellions' attack accounted for," I say, tapping the spreadsheet with my pen. "But what's the timeline on actually getting the construction completed? You guys have been having church at the Ridge for over a month."

Gunnar leans back in his chair, running a hand over his beard. "Hard to say. With the amount of damage, we're looking at a major overhaul. Luckily, X's buddy Holt owns a damn good construction company in town."

I nod, recalling the name. "Kavanaugh Development, right? I've heard good things about them."

"Exactly," Gunnar affirms. "Holt's been a solid friend to the club for years. We've tried getting him to prospect, but he's always been hesitant to commit fully."

"What if the club offered to invest in his company? It could be a mutually beneficial arrangement. We get priority for the compound repairs, and he gets a financial boost for his business."

Gunnar strokes his beard contemplatively.

"That's not a bad idea. Holt's a good guy with a solid business, and it would strengthen our ties with him. Plus, we could use some of the funds from taking down Moretti to finance the investment."

"Precisely," I agree, excited by the prospect. "It's a way to put that money to good use while also securing a reliable construction partner."

Gunnar nods thoughtfully. "I like it. We should run it by Rex, get his thoughts on the idea."

"Of course," I agree. "It's his call as President to have the club vote on it."

Gunnar flashes me a grateful smile.

"You've been a godsend, Anna. I don't know how I managed it all before you came on board."

"I'm just glad I can contribute something meaningful to the club."

I jump as a shadow fills my doorway. Relieved when I see it's only Rex. His hands rest on the top of the door frame, his body slightly leaning forward into the doorway. One lingering look between us speaks volumes of his unspoken intensions. Gunnar turns to see what has caught my attention behind him.

"We were just talking about a potential investment we wanted to run by you," Gunnar explains.

Rex shakes his head. "Later, get out." His tone leaves no room for argument.

Gunnar pauses before standing up and making his way to the door. Once he is out of the room, Rex reaches behind him and closes the door, locking it securely.

My heart races as Rex slowly stalks across the room. Closing the distance between us like a hunter stalks his prey. Our eyes meet and I'm frozen in place by the intensity of his stare.

Rex rounds the desk, his muscular frame towering over me. Rex's broad shoulders and chest strain against the fabric of his black tee shirt, stretching tightly, outlining each muscle with precision. His arms are thick and bulging, the veins standing out like raised highways along his arms.

I can hear Rex's deep breaths as he stands over me, his chest rising and falling with each inhale and exhale. I swallow hard, feeling both nervous and captivated. Without a word, he grips the arms of my chair, caging me in between them and his powerful body. The scent of his cologne mixed with leather, whiskey, and something purely masculine surrounds me, subtle and inviting.

"Anna," his voice rough and deep like gravel, sends a wave of heat through me.

I hold my breath as Rex moves closer, our foreheads almost touching. His intense gaze locks onto mine, making me feel fully exposed in a deliciously vulnerable way.

Rex's rough, work-worn hands grab onto my hair, tilting my head back, bringing my face closer to him. He tilts my head to the side, his lips trailing kisses from just below my ear, down the curve of my neck. A soft moan escapes me as he nips at my skin with his teeth, only to soothe it quickly with the warmth of his tongue as it slides across my skin.

My nails scrape against the solid muscles of his chest as he pulls me closer. A low rumble escapes from deep within Rex’s throat as he stands up straight. I let out a surprised breath as Rex swiftly clears my desk with one powerful sweep, sending papers and files scattering to the floor.

Before I can even react, he is lifting me up from my office chair. Turning me around so that I am now facing my desk. "Rex," my voice trembling with excitement. "What are you doing?"

He stays silent, his breath is hot against my neck as he bends me over the desk. He places one hand between my shoulders to gently guide me down as the other firmly grips my hip before snaking down to the hem of my skirt. He bunches my skirt up around my waist, exposing me to him. An involuntary whimper escapes my lips, as his fingers slowly glide across my skin, tracing the curve of my ass.

"Rex," I gasp, my voice hoarse with need.

He remains silent, his focus entirely on the task at hand. I whimper again as he drops to his knees behind me, his fingers hooking into the waistband of my panties.

My body trembles with desire as I weakly protest, "Rex, we can't do this here."

He ignores my protest, as he slowly slides my panties down my legs. I step out of them, trying to keep my composure as I brace myself against the desk's edge.

"Anna, I can do any damn thing I want, anywhere I want," Rex growls, his voice low and seductive.

His fingers move along the sensitive skin of my inner thighs, leaving behind a trail of goosebumps in their wake. I moan softly, my knees buckling slightly as he moves with a teasing slowness. His fingers barely grazing where I crave his touch the most, leaving me aching and desperate for more.

"And today baby, I decided I wanted my dessert before dinner."

His words send a thrill of excitement coursing through me. I lean forward eagerly against the desk as Rex's warm breath caresses my sensitive skin. He begins devouring my pussy hungrily. His skilled tongue tracing long, deliberate, paths from my throbbing clit to the entrance of my ass, circling and teasing my tight hole. My body responds immediately, arching and writhing as pleasure washes over me.

Rex's big hands move around to the front of my thighs griping them tightly, pulling me back onto him as his tongue delves deeper into my core. I can't control the desperate movements of my hips as I thrust back, fucking myself on his tongue, against his mouth, craving more of him.

Sweat glistens on my skin, my voice hoarse and desperate. "Oh, God, Rex," I moaned, my hands clutching at the edge of the desk beneath me. Searching for anything to hold onto to anchor myself. "Don't stop, please."

He chuckles, the vibration of his deep laugh against my skin sending shivers down my body.

"I'm just getting started, baby, and I'm a hungry fuckin' man."

I moaned loudly as pleasure surged through me. Rex's strong fingers grip my thighs tighter, spreading them wider, while his tongue flicks against my throbbing clit in a steady rhythm. My body trembles with pleasure, building towards an explosive orgasm.

"Rex, I'm going to come."

Rex pulls away, "not yet, turn around." I do as he says, his hands gently guiding me to turn around and face him. I follow his lead, sitting on the edge of my desk.

"Take your shirt and bra off," he instructs in a commanding tone. His eyes are ravenous as he watches me hungrily as I remove my tank top tossing it to the floor. I unclasp the front hook of my bra and my breasts spill free. The cool air on my heated skin causing my nipples to pebble. His eyes roam over my body as he takes hold of my legs, parting them slowly and spreading me open wide before him like a precious treasure. He places the heels of my feet on the edge of the desk, positioning me exactly how he desires.

“Eyes on me, you close them or look away… I’ll fucking stop.” His voice demanding, dripping with dominance making me want him even more.

He slides two thick fingers inside me, agonizingly slow, deliberately teasing me.

“Always so wet for me,” his voice raspy with desire. “Been craving the taste of you on my tongue all fucking day.”

Rex leans in and brushing a soft kiss on my inner thigh, so close to where I ache for his touch. My body shakes as he inches his tongue towards my clit, teasingly circling around but not actually making contact. I can't help but buck my hips, begging for more of him.

“Please.”

He looks up at me with a predatory smile playing on his lips. “Please what?”

“Plea...” I trail off, not even sure of what I'm asking for.

His smile widens, “You have to beg me, pretty girl.”

Those words made my insides clench with need. “Please, Rex,” I beg, my cheeks flaming with embarrassment.

His grin widens further, "Beg me a little louder."

"Oh, God, Rex! Please... please just fucking make me come."

As soon as the words leave my mouth, the grin falls from his face and he eagerly dives in, his tongue hungrily lapping at my throbbing clit. He devours me like his life depends on it. My hands grip Rex's hair tightly, holding him against me as an orgasm threatens to consume me.

"Rex, I can't..." My head falls back and my eyes close.

Rex stops, his voice stern. "What did I tell you Anna? Keep those beautiful fucking eyes open and watch me eat your pussy, or I'll stop again. If I have to stop again, I won't finish."

I open my eyes, meeting his smirking gaze. His eyes dark pools swirling with lust and hunger. He's enjoying this, every damn second of my torture, and I've never been more turned on in my life.

"That's it baby, watch me make you come apart for me."

His words, husky with desire, have an instant effect, and I feel my body trembling on the edge once more. Rex, sensing my desperation, knows exactly what I need. He increases the speed, his tongue and fingers working together in tandem to bring me to the brink of oblivion. My nails scratch at the wooden desk as I try to hold on to any semblance of control I have left.

“Rex... I...”

“Play with your nipples. Show me how you like it." Releasing my grip on the desk, my hands slowly sliding up my body. His eyes track the movement as I follow his command. Tracing the outline of my breasts with my fingertips before gently rolling and pinching my nipples until they become hard peaks between my fingers. He watched intently, a deep growl rumbling in his chest.

"Harder," he demands, his breath hot against my dripping sex. I obey, squeezing and pulling at my nipples, moaning at the delicious pain that shoots straight to my core.

“That’s it, baby. Now be a good girl and watch as I finger fuck you and make you come on my tongue.”

My body trembles as he teases me, his fingers trailing along my thighs. Then he plunges them inside me, hitting all the right spots. I moaned as he sucked hard on my clit. I watched him, his head between my parted legs, his warm tongue swirling around my clit. I never took my eyes off him as he made me come undone.

“Fuck! Rex!” I scream as the orgasm crashes into me, ripping me apart at the seams. My nails leave crescent shaped indents on the skin of my breasts as my back arches, and I ride out the most intense orgasm of my life.

Rex looks up at me, a cocky smile spread across his lips. “Sweetest fuckin’ thing I’ve ever tasted,” he says while running his tongue over his mouth, licking his lips clean. Rising to his feet, he peels off his shirt with a slow, seductive grace. His hands glide down toned muscles and inked skin to the buckle of his belt, teasingly undoing the clasp before sliding the zipper of his jeans down.

Rex hooks a thumb in the waistband of his jeans and boxers. Pushing them down until they fall to the floor freeing his thick cock. He stood before me like a living sculpture. His towering, muscular body was a masterpiece of strength and definition. Every muscle and line chiseled to perfection.

“Tell me you want this.” His eyes were locked on mine, as he gripped his cock. I watch, unable to tear my eyes away as his hand moves, slowly sliding up and down his hard shaft as he strokes himself.

“I want it,” I pant, my cheeks flushing red with desire. He grips the base of his cock tightly as he rubs the broad head through my wet pussy, teasing my entrance with each pass.

“Tell me you’re mine,” Rex growls, the fingers of his free hand digging into my hip.

“I’m yours,” My breath catches in my throat as he thrusts his cock deep inside of me. Pleasure surges through my body. I cling to him, my nails digging into his broad shoulders.

Rex buries his face in my neck, “fuuuck,” he moans in my ear. “I love the way your pussy grips my cock. You feel so fucking good.” My nails scrape across his back as he fucks me against the desk. He nips at my neck, “say it again, baby. Say you’re mine.”

And in that moment, as our bodies collided, Rex took me to heights I never knew possible, I knew he was mine just as much as I was his.

"I'm yours, Rex. Only yours." I moaned, my climax building again. His grip tightens around my hips, pulling me back onto his cock as he thrusts up into me hard. He buries himself deep inside with one final thrust, spilling inside of me. His body shaking with the force of his orgasm as he collapses against me, on top the desk.

We stay there, lying across my desk until we both catch our breaths.

"Rex?"

"Yeah?"

"When I told you in bed this morning that I had a fantasy of you taking me on my desk… I wasn't expecting you to have me spread eagle seven hours later across it."

I could feel him shaking with laughter against my body. "Lucky for you, I always aim to please."

* * *

Rex walks into our bedroom, after tucking Em into bed for the night. I take a deep breath, trying to build up my courage. I've been waiting for the right moment for a few days to bring this up.

"There was something I wanted to run past you."

Rex looks up at me with those intense blue eyes that always make my heart skip a beat. "What's on your mind, baby? This about the investment for the club Gunnar mentioned earlier?"

I fidget with the edge of the blanket, suddenly feeling unsure. "No, it's not about that."

He nods, giving me his full attention. "Okay, so what is it then?"

"Sarah, my mom, and I were talking, and after spending so much time with Aria and Bree and seeing their progress and how far they've come, we were thinking about opening a shelter for trafficking and abuse victims. We wanted to ask the club if we could use some of the money that was recovered from the Moretti's."

Rex remains silent, his expression unreadable as he processes what I've said.

I rush to continue, the words tumbling out. "I know it's a lot to ask, but could we build the shelter inside the compound as part of the rebuild from the attack? I've never felt safer in my life than the time I've spent here with the club and all the guys. We all feel the same way. I want the women and children we help to feel that too."

A small smile tugs at the corner of Rex's mouth. "Baby, I think that's one hell of a way to spend that money, making those bastards pay for what they had a hand in breaking."

Hope blooms in my chest, but Rex holds up a hand, tempering my excitement.

"But it's not just up to me. It's a club decision whether to allow it or not. And if it's on the compound, that shelter won't just belong to you women. It will belong to the club if it's on club property, but you guys can run it how you see fit as long as it’s not interfering with club business."

I can't help the squeal of excitement that escapes my lips, and Rex chuckles.

"Hold on now," he says, his tone sobering. "It's far from a done deal. A shelter like that could bring a world of problems on the club. The wrong person comes looking to take back what they see as theirs could be bad for everyone involved. But I'll take it to the table. I think you girls can do a fuck of a lot of good."

His support meant the world to me, but I knew the club's decision wasn't guaranteed.

"I understand," I said, trying to keep my voice steady. "Thank you for being willing to bring it to the table."

"You and the girls have done a lot for us. The least the club can do is consider it."

"Thank you," I whisper to Rex as he pulls me into a tight hug. "You have no idea how much this means."

His arms tighten around me. "Even if the club votes against a shelter being built within the compound, I'll still make this happen for you if it's what you want. This is your chance to turn everything you went through into something good, baby. Make it count."

I leaned into his touch, feeling a wave of gratitude. "You're amazing, you know that?"

He smirked, his thumb brushing my cheek. "I know."

I laughed softly, the tension easing from my shoulders. I know there may be difficult times ahead, but I've never felt more certain that I'm exactly where I belong.

THE END

Connect With Gracie

I'd love to have you join my reader group on Facebook. You'll get all the dirt on new releases and sneak peaks before anyone else.

Follow me on Facebook, Instagram, or Goodreads.

I have open spots on my ARC team. If you would be interested in joining my ARC Team or Street Team, you can fill out the form here.

OTHER BOOKS IN THIS SERIES

Retribution

Book 1

Vengeance

Book 2

Printed in Great Britain
by Amazon

48031169R00169